A.N. Irvano was born in California in 1990, and
continues to live in the area.
This is the author's first novel.

Falling Horse Books

Chicken River Dance

Chicken River Dance

A.N.Irvano

Falling Horse Books

Chicken River Dance

Copyright © 2014 A.N.Irvano

First Edition

Book Design: A.N. Irvano

ISBN: 978-0-9960346-0-9

Printed in the United States of America

As a child, I spent so many countless hours reading books that when I would lift my hands afterwards, they would sometimes feel as light as balloons. I grew stronger each time I held the immense weight that every book has the propensity to carry. I want to thank my parents and parents like them for putting the weight of the world into the hands of their children and helping them grow to be strong enough to carry it.

-A.

Chapter One

Sitting in my own silence, I became acutely alert to
the noises my relatives had grown accustomed to. The
pressing hands of a small clock moved with diminutive
thunks. The ice maker and refrigerator competed for
sonic space as they made their respective hums in the
kitchen. Above me, from the bedrooms, came noises of
the house shifting slowly in the autumnal wind of the
night. The day would not break.

A presence in the house had been agitated, I
thought. The recent news had upset me, making my
perception of the home somehow different. The recent
call from my father about my cousins' lives, and their
deaths, was heavy in my mind. I worried now for my
father, who had driven to my aunt's house and searched
for meaning where there was none.

No less than five hours ago he had asked me to come
from my apartment in the Bay to his house in the inland
suburbs because of my cousins. They had been killed, he
said. I did not doubt or question, unconcerned with
anything but the intuitive response to protect my family.
Having driven down the coast to find nobody home had

threatened to conceal my good sense. Agitated at all I had learned, I walked around the empty house with its ticking timepieces. The day would not break no matter how much time the clocks kept.

To keep myself calm, I touched the old objects my ancestors had, searching their work and portraits for fragments of familiar characteristics or features. I saw myself nearly fully in the candid photographs of my mother, lined up on a shelf perpendicular to images of my aunt. I asked myself to feel sympathy for my aunt, but my spirit was skeptical. I hadn't seen the way their bodies were placed after their deaths.

Troubled as I was in that moment, the news hadn't yet shaken me to my core. It hadn't yet asked me to shed tears, spit up bile, and wrack my brain with the question of what I had to do to help them, or to save them. But that was because I didn't know anything about it, yet. The day would not break no matter how much I willed it.

My body fell asleep in an empty rectangle of space between the clocks. I was awoken in the dark hour before dawn.

My father shook my shoulder with his hand. "Ryan, this is one of the most important things you can do today." From above me, he said, "Go downtown and go to the only cafe with trees and seating in front of it, a block away from the water, called Insight Cafe." He blinked at me and I nodded before he spoke again, "There you'll find Jake, you both need to go over to Angelique's house today."

"I want a little more information than that," I said hotly.

He sighed, rubbing his temples with one hand, and said, "Your cousins have all been murdered. I don't know by who, but after going to their house and finding out that your mom is gone, it made me realize I never will, but Jake will. He's a very close friend. It's important you find out more with him. Please go." He moved quietly into his office, where papers I had never seen before had been systematically piled. He flicked his large, dark hand at me to get out as he noticed my straining eyes. I noticed how my hands had begun to resemble his as I aged. I had to look down at them and see how much of my father I was turning into as I grabbed my keys and was out the door.

The drive was not one I knew well but the car was. It took turns well and fast and the bucket racing seats created an impenetrable stronghold between me and the road. Trying to find the apex of every turn was a challenge that put my mind at rest. A great and overbearing sense of my lack of knowledge took hold and incessantly tore at my emotions.

I tried appeasing my fear for my mother by going over the things I knew about her. She was bright and vivacious and whenever I could see her, my day was brightened. She had made me a safe place when I was born, even if it was far from her, and I could always trust her to make sure I wasn't harmed. She took me out as often as possible since they had set up a house close to them. My father, on the other hand, stayed inside with me and allowed me only the benefits of reading his books or talking over an issue with him.

The only cafe downtown bearing a sign had an expansive front. Trees lined the sidewalk next to it and there was seating outside. My favorite cafe in Oakland's

Lower Bottoms came quickly to my mind in contrasting recollection. The cafe here was pristine, standing with absolute certainty of its importance against the sidewalk. The cafe I knew in Oakland seemed almost ashamed as it leaned away from the Bay Area's rapid transit lines, which thundered with the power of passing trains like a football stadium would thunder after a good play. As the day had only just begun, people were milling in and out of this small town's cafe quickly, ready to start now that they had their coffee in hand.

When I went in a pale man with protruding teeth greeted me quickly by saying, "Hello and such, what can I get you?"

"Jake," I said as he pushed an eyebrow up, "I need to speak with him. I actually need to take Jake."

He swung around to face a second man with lady eyebrows and a ginger man's beard. "Jake, this young boy said he would like to, 'take Jake.' The nerve!" His eyes widened at me frivolously and then turned to the man he had presumably been talking to. Jake swung around to face us, but only listened to the pale man speak, "I didn't ask if it's going to be through the front or back, but here he is, ready and waiting."

Jake smiled ashamedly and said, "Victor, nothing nice to say today?"

Words flooded my mouth before I was ready for them, then tumbled out, "Was that a joke, 'take Jake.'? You made a sex joke? There's been some. . ."

Jake moved past Victor and asked, "What can you not say?"

My voice shook as I responded, "Murders." I liked jokes, I even quite especially found sex jokes funny. A good facetiae almost always had a place in conversation. I would have even liked to make a witticism right then. Why I scolded him, I didn't know. My legs shook as I stepped closer to Jake. He tamped out some espresso, turned to a young girl sitting at the bar, and spoke a few words to her, at which she got up and pushed in behind the bar to take the espresso head from his hands and plug it into the machine. He walked to her seat at the bar and gestured for me to sit down.

Jake said, "So what's the problem? You've just said some big things have happened which I am not aware of. Fill me in, young one?"

"My dad, Herman Hull, asked me to get you after he visited the crime scene of my cousins' deaths. I got here just last night."

"All six of them?" The girl working the espresso machines looked at me as she interjected. Her eyes were so aggressive that I felt searched and demoralized after she had asked me.

"Yes, I at least think so. I haven't been privy to everything." I said as I watched the girl turn around and eye me up and down, "Anything actually."

Before speaking, Jake gestured to the girl to turn back around and to face away from us. "Ah, of course not. But should you be?" He shook his head and grimaced before watching a corner of the room for a moment. I shrugged and pondered his rhetorical question aimlessly. He took his eyes away from the far off place they had been to gaze at me. In a manner completely dissimilar from the girl's, he looked at me politely.

"Where have you been living and for how long?" he asked me. I felt a desire to hide some of what I told him about myself in my answer.

"Bay Area, but only for four months," I told him.

"Ah, well they didn't even think to tell me you existed. Your parents are liars!" he exclaimed at me as he rubbed his legs with his hands and moved up angrily.

I asked, "Excuse me?" I felt I had failed at hiding enough information to make him happy.

"Only testing what you think of them." His sharp, thin eyebrows quickly gestured as he spoke.

Realizing we both knew little, I became honest, "But about these, my cousins, my dad doesn't seem to know enough about that and so he wanted you." Jake breathed in a way that made his cheeks balloon out to where his curling, twisted beard started as he listened.

"He used to be so sharp, your father," he said. "Sometimes people will grab at pre-existing thought processes, thinking the current problem calls and demands for them when really what they need is to come up with something completely different."

I thought about that enough to ask, "Is that what he's doing here, going to a friend he's comfortable with for help? And you think that's wrong?"

He lifted himself from the bar with the determination of a man getting old, himself. "I actually think we should find out. You tell me some stories on the way there. That way I don't get bored with your lack of intel about the issues at hand. Okay?"

"I don't usually tell stories," I said to him as he waved goodbye to patrons.

He patted Victor's large back, saying, "Take care of things here, Victor." Then said to me, "Education begins a gentlemen, conversation completes him. Thomas Fuller originally said that, but I'll apply it."

"I don't know if you have noticed," I said, holding out the pale palms of my hands and flipping them over to show the stark black contrast of the back of them, "But I'm not often seen as a possessing the appropriate qualities of a genteel man."

He frowned, "Sure you are."

"Good to know you're above putting others down."

"So you do have stories."

"Some of them don't need to be mulled over too much."

"Ah, but they'll give me some insight about you. I think I'll be getting to know you quite well," he retorted.

"When I was in boarding school I heard about-" I began, but he objected by interrupting.

"You what?" he exclaimed loudly, "Why were you there?"

I started the drive slower than I had done when I had driven there alone, without this vociferating man in the car, "When my mom gave birth to me, she thought she wouldn't be fit to take care of me. She was worried about the way it would work with her, uh, well, she was worried about creating division in her own ranks."

"That's one reason, but not all of them." he said. "You don't get everything you want all throughout your lifetime, you know."

"My lifetime has been this care school program that basically boarded me, raised me, and taught me. When she was pregnant she thought it would be a burden to have a child at the beginning of their careers. They were still together, in a way, my mom and father. They said they were fluid and dynamic and were together when it was appropriate." I stopped myself when I felt winded but Jake held onto the thought with his fingers stroking one another.

He let out a soft whisper of words, "And do you feel anything about that?"

"I don't feel about it. I think about it, though," I said to him.

"So you hold back your emotional side," he spoke hungrily and I got a sense that he didn't act on the words he spoke, "and let your analytical one take over?"

I felt uncomfortable giving too little information, "I tend to feel less, because I've opened up to thinking more. So, yes, something like that."

"Many people have the problem of letting their emotional side take over. Pardon me for saying, many women do that and many men do that because of women. Some men, like me, do it because of other men, too." I glanced at him next to me, "Your mother, in particular, did not let her emotions take over. You would have been in plenty of danger had you stayed close to your parents as you grew up. But you, you take after your father by shielding what your logical side does not want to see. That is also why we should see quite quickly why he has done that today."

"You mean this isn't like him?" I asked.

"You have not had the time to sit down with him often, understand him?" he asked about my father.

"No, not particularly. I think I know him, though," he looked at me as I spoke and I peered back at him, wondering what I didn't know. My father had not shown me who I was, what I wanted, and how to get it, all without hurting me. Not yet. Would we get a chance, though?

"You may. You are very much like him, at least. You may get to know him by knowing more about yourself. You may get to know him through these events. Or you may reject him altogether. Working out issues with your father is not the pinnacle of your life. Drive faster, please. I want to hear about this," he said. "No, do not drive to your parents. Go to your mom's sister's, she's a tortured woman right now, but that's where we need to learn what happened."

None of my family was in front of the one-story house, but a few huge holes in the ground were, as well as a terribly sweet smell in the air. The ground leading to the porch had huge mounds that had been piled next to a narrow walkway. We side-stepped them entirely by making a beeline for the side of the house. We had to grab at the wood of the porch and house to make it in. Jake groped mechanically at the steps and I grabbed his hand and pulled him on, helping him avoid the mounds.

He gasped at the porch and sniffed the air, "Smell funny to you?" I sniffed the dirt but it was not the cause. He shrugged and went inside.

I gazed at the sight and realized the dirt wasn't dry on the top layer and must have been dug up and piled recently. I shook my head, wondering why there would be open rectangular holes in the lawn.

The door was ajar, but I was beyond it quickly, following in Jake's steps. A gathering of uniformed officers blockaded our way at first, but stepped back when they saw the both of us wordlessly entering. Jake raised a hand and they parted even more for us to make our way.

The hallway had the same remarkable smell of sweetness. It clung to my nostrils, forcing images of cotton candy, ice cream, and sleeping outside in the summer. Blowing out my nose didn't help, so I let the smell linger along with the fleeting associations flickering through my mind.

Each door from the hall had a small layer of police tape blockading it. The kitchen in the back was inhabited by my aunt who was sitting at the table with balled-up fists in her hair. Emotional barricades had been constructed along her face, popping out the veins on her temple and creating a raw line of rage and sadness across her eyes.

Jake sat down quietly next to her and let her know he was there with a gentle touch on the shoulder. He said, "Something to know is that I'm here to learn what happened, because I don't like it and I'm here to help. Rachelle's husband was here earlier and he wants me to see what's here now, but before I look can you tell me everything, down to the last detail?"

Angelique looked up to him with pale eyes. I noticed how the brown of her irises faded into the white. Clear tears ran down her shallow brown cheeks. She cried out when she tried to say my mother's name.

Jake put another arm around her and they both shuddered and cringed out grief together.

She finally said, "Rachelle, she noticed the horses were loose around one o'clock. We were both still up, here in the dining room, talking, and we could hear them in the canyon. So she went after them."

Jake interjected quickly, "Did she take a car or walk?"

She pushed her eyebrows together, "I would have to check out front," she shook her head, "I didn't hear anything."

"Don't you have dogs?" he asked.

She put up her arm as her neck failed to keep up her head and said, "Two."

"Strange that the dogs didn't bark, either." Jake mused, "It is curious."

Her head shook with sobs as she said, "They're gone, too!"

Jake's eyes moved swiftly across the room, like he was reading a newspaper very quickly. "Rachelle left, then what did you do?"

Tears swelled out of her eyes like garden water from a green hose. Her veins along the temple and close to her eyes tumefied and I thought of the tendons inside the human heart that went from ceiling to wall and stayed taught. Deep emotional trauma could loosen them and they would weaken.

Words stumbled out of her mouth and she said, "I checked on my kids. None of them were there, Jake. So I ran out to the front, to call for them. That's when I saw them. They were buried right there in front of the house, each one of their faces popping out of the dirt." Her words were harsh rasps as they made their way out, "Their faces were," she strained her eyes to a distant place, "looking up at me, like they were waiting for me to come save them. Their tiny faces were there, just like they were coming out of me. But they weren't. They were-" she faltered and stopped speaking to make room for heart-wracking sobs.

Jake said, "I'm sorry I have to ask, but their father is where?"

She sighed and an old, painful trio of words sprung out of her mouth, "He is dead."

"May we go to the rooms?" Jake asked. She nodded and he stood. I followed suit.

As we entered the hallway, Jake's voice boomed, "That smell, that incredible, unplaceable smell! Is it a fragrance you have here often? Do any of your children have asthma or inhalers?"

Angelique came into the first room with us, dabbing a tissue to her eyes, "No. Never. I noticed the taste in my mouth when I was running between the rooms, looking for them." She shuddered a sob into her tissue. Jake sighed with her concern, for it was in his eyes, too.

Jake held himself high, looking over the room in its entirety. Only after he looked with his eyes, then bent at the waist to look by the beds, did he speak, pointing between the two beds, "See here, this depression in the carpet?" He looked at it closely and took a pen out of his pocket, taking measurements, before pointing again to a corner of the room, "See the dirt on the wall and carpet is the same kind as the stuff dug fresh outside. That's not any top layer stuff that your kids would have brought in from outside." He got closer, looked closer. "That's what the diggers brought in. By the looks of it they were leaning against the wall, here." He looked around the room much more quickly now, then finally settling on Angelique, "Next room."

"Ah, same feature in the carpet. It is quite obvious they had some kind of machine sitting here." He stood and looked at her, concerned.

"I will check on you in a few days, but for now tell us anything about Rachelle before we leave. Be specific about what she took when she left," his voice was softer as he spoke. Angelique looked furtively from me to her hands and I straightened my jaw, worried about my mom immediately.

"I watched her take that bag she takes to Herman's," she said slowly, with conviction.

His voice was softer as he spoke, "What do you think was going through her mind?"

"She heard the noises first as we were talking around the table. She went out the front door, Jake." As she spoke her face grew convoluted with emotions. Her hands trembled above her lap and I wondered how much longer we had to torment her with questions. Jake shook his head and kept his mouth closed, to my relief.

My aunt slammed her fists on the table, the tissue splaying under one of them, and said, "She had to have chased the ones that did it!" Starting with my fists and feet, my body pulsed with an urge to tear from the house, past the graves.

Jake stood up, drawing himself closer to me, and asked Angelique, "Is that something you've told the police?"

"She told me to never disclose her actions to anyone outside of Herman and yourself. I wish I could have actually told Herman this, but I've been," a soft murmur was all that escaped her, "very emotionally weak since I found them. I couldn't have even talked to him. I guess I blamed him. This profession they're in, it's no way to live. They've ruined a family!" Larger sobs encompassed her words after that, making her impossible to understand, or even to look at. I forced myself to look at her, though, dubious as to what my mother and dad were doing to put my cousins in danger.

Jake wrapped his hands around my shoulders. "Ryan, I want you to go ahead to your car while I study the scene a bit more. Angelique, before was some of the most lucid and level-headed thinking I've heard in a long time. Let's let you start talking about how you feel now."

"Thank you," she said, and more of the sobs that had been pressing to get out released themselves.

I walked from the house and in the breaking daylight the graves that had been covered over in the night were now empty and fresh once more. Each child-shaped hole carried in it the marks of death. I was overcome. I bent over as tears and bile fell from my face. I thought to push both back in order to look around, since the great mass of soil that had been dug up blocked most of the police officers from seeing, but when a third substance, snot, mingled with the tears and spit draining from me, I got on my knees, threw my hands to my face, and gave up trying to control my emotions.

Life had taught me to be rational, aware, and flexible to what I saw and could learn. These events, these murders, were showing me that there were some things I did not need to accept. There was no rationalization, no way I could explain this intent as just one more problem to solve. The people that had done this had as little excuse as I had, and yet they did. We both possessed the ability to destroy, but only they had carried it out. I reasoned that I was not a person that could. That didn't stop the hateful thoughts that spiraled down to this: find them, destroy them. I felt the pain brand itself within me, lurking and aware of atrocities I could not fix.

Jake and I drove back and I saw the area around my relative's house was set in a soft glow. Strung lights on the street and the gleam of sunrise filtered from the mountains in the East, where there were fewer homes and towns. From inside the house I grabbed my laptop bag and the overnight duffel I had brought from

Berkeley. I was leaving this town, finding my mom, finding out about these killers that were perhaps after her.

My father was on the landing and said, "I was able to see the children before they were exhumed. Would you like to know what killed them?"

I said, "Yes, I would."

"Poisoned with Artheum. A new chemical agent that was proving very successful in a few studies. This is the first time it has been tested for this purpose."

"I want to find them. You can, right?"

He shook his head. His hands went to his temples and he walked down the steps as he spoke, "Son, as you age, you gain new thought processes, but you also lose some as well. The thought processes you have at your disposal at any present moment are what will guide you to success. I have substantially less than I should. Less than you."

"I wouldn't say I have more than you. You can make an algorithm out of theory. Mom said you were once able to get into a headmaster's private bedroom with a hairpin you took off of his wife's head. You're amazing."

He sighed as he walked toward me, "You're amazing, too."

I felt clear about the great and vast nothingness I had, hoping it would persuade my father from his self-destructive grievances. I hadn't done more than three months of one thing, ranging in too wide array to say I was close to his alleged amazing. I was not close to awe-inducing, or awesome, I was barely able to put my pants on everyday and keep doing the simple intricacies of life.

"I'm nothing." I told him, "All I am is what you've given me."

"People stop learning. Their potential for growth is halted and soon they are simply going through the motions of pressing the buttons of what they knew before and applying that information." He raised a hand and let it fall on my shoulder, "I have stopped learning, unlike you, my son." I shook my head but he continued to talk. "Never stop gathering information. I believe in you more than I believe in myself."

I made my question a statement, "Can we talk about what's actually happening."

"I want you to do this one for me. I want you to find out. You are so much more capable than me. And with Rachelle gone, who knows why, but I can't wrap my own feelings for this case up well enough to go after it." I shook my head, holding his gaze, and he rubbed my shoulder softly, speaking steadily, "I've been working against a brain tumor for a few years and can't push myself into this one, but I can give you the facts." He raised his arm and ushered me into his office to the table where he had splayed out papers.

"I can't—" I began. He raised a hand.

"Have I told you I'm a detective? We both are," he said and patted the table.

"-do this." My hands fell to my side and my knees gave a series of tremors.

He said, "Probably the reason Rachelle is missing is linked to the detective work we've been doing. Think about this as a code for you to crack. A code to hack." At these words, I knew he knew all about me.

"You know I can program?"

"I know you can hack."

"You know there's more to it than just that word, right?" I asked, trying to step on a pedestal he couldn't get on.

He laughed, "I know all about the families of any girls you've dated, your favorite brand of candy. I know a good deal. Remember what I'm telling you now. I'm a professional detective and your father, you couldn't go many places without me knowing what you were doing."

I told him, "When I was train hopping, though, you had no idea."

He gave a deep chuckle, "Oh, yes we did. Your mom even found out you were about to get that tattoo. Hated that. That's why we got you those plane tickets and the apartment. She was keeping closer tabs on you during that time than me and the minute you had a conversation with that beard-o about getting a tattoo, she went insane with worry."

I felt an inward chuckle that I did not let slip past my lips. This was so much to hold onto. I was facing the truth. I spoke quickly, "You're insane for thinking you can have me go to find her now. Alone, no less!"

"Don't make me pull out the good old your-mother-is-missing card. Just know that I can. You're going with Jake today to find her," he smiled and tapped on the table to a picture of a man, "and him."

"Who is he?" I asked.

"He's been the biggest new technology weapons dealer on the West Coast for half a decade," he said. "Mentored into the position, too. He's not good, he's great." The man in the picture had ribbons for wrinkles, deep fjords cracked into the skin between and above his eyebrows, next to his eyes, across his chin. He had no laugh lines, no sensitive glimmer in his eyes, none of the features I had grown to admire.

My father said his name, "Leonard Kiljun. We caught video surveillance from our buddies that had their warehouse robbed of the machines Artheum is used in. He was pulling strings and a group of about five did the job. I'm assuming the same group carried out the events at your aunt's. There really is no reason for burying them." He covered his face in his hands as he bent down to rest his elbows on the picture.

"Especially with their faces exposed." I said, "They didn't work hard to cover them up."

"No, they didn't. Maybe there was a motive for that." He scratched his head then began, again, "Now, Artheum is beyond my expertise; I never was a chemist." He pulled out a paper that showed chemical bonds and said, "But I understand they are working with a class of gasses that force actions. Some of their most popular actually provide nourishment to the body, energize a person, et cetera. Some of their most lethal have been used on your cousins. I saw that the area around their noses was red, like they had had breathing masks on. So, I swabbed and found powdery residue on their nostrils and mouths, cross-analyzed it with samples. I realized a robbery was linked up. They were using the same chemicals and inhalers that were stolen just last night." My nose pricked, remembering the sweet smell in the house.

"Who's this?" I asked, pointing to another very pale, white man with thin lips and tiny, shark eyes.

"Carlyle Bruisyn," he said.

"I'm getting a bad feeling off of this guy."

He looked at me speculatively, then pushed his hands back against his temples. "Why the band of robbers are insane enough to test their theory on our family is very important for me to know. It was very intentional."

He raised his eyes to me, sighed, and drew a cigarette pack out of his pocket. He slowly tapped the cigarette against the table, pushing the tobacco towards the filter, before lighting it. His eyes fixed on the crisp photos. The smell of his cigarette reminded me of the past happy year I had spent smoking and socializing. Now the acrid smell burnt my nose and made my head reel and churn with vicious thoughts.

"She gave me up to protect me. Why wouldn't she distance herself from Angelique too?"

"Rachelle moved out of her immediate family's lives when she was twenty-five, very young. For a very long time she was removed from her family. These past few months she and I decided to do a bit of retiring. Settling down and getting back in touch, so to speak." He looked nervously at me as he spoke, not knowing where to place me in their lives, "We should have never done that."

"What exactly makes you think I can do this? I don't need validation, don't placate me. I just do not think I'm going to be able to solve the missing-mom mystery. My missing mom. How is the extremity of this situation lost on you?"

"The young have an advantage over the old because they have a greater capability for expansion. Being better than the generations before you is one of your strong suits."

"What about mom?"

He put a hand on my shoulder and tapped it as he shifted his body and spoke, "Rachelle may be where the heat is going to happen. She's also likely stalking those that killed them, your poor cousins." His hand faltered near his leg and grasped onto the table as he bent over. "Or she's still in the canyon, doesn't know anything about any of this, and is just riding till the cows come home, likely tonight." He looked up at me with a fresh smile, "Praise hope."

"Were you just making a joke?"

"Never could reach out to the younger generation, could I?"

"You're not doing it now, that's for sure."

"I'm less youthful than-"

"Are you okay?"

"I really am not feeling well. Have I said that yet?" I suddenly had to jump up from my chair to catch him. He spoke again before letting himself fall into a seat, "Don't call a doctor, don't worry. This happens with stress, agitation. Do the thing. Jake is more helpful than me, now, go. . . go."

I heard Jake at the front door, yoo-hooing that he was there. I called out to him, "Can you help my dad?"

"What's happened?" he said as he rushed in.

"Just a— Oh, Dad. A brain tumor! That's what he's got going on. Nothing, right?"

"Let me have a minute with him," he said softly, again showing appropriate concern.

Walking away from the house without starting to accept the consequences of what I was leaving behind was my first act of alienation of the day. We human beings are the most selfish of all, becoming distressed when someone's sick or dying because they are no longer around for us. I thought about that and thought how selfless I would have been if I were to be concerned with what I could no longer give to them once they were dead. Even less self-centered than that would be a concern for them no longer being able to receive anything the world had to offer, now that they were dead.

Chapter Two

Jake's once-eager face was now solemn as we drove away from both houses. I ran into the cafe only to see the large man from earlier still behind the register, pressing buttons with no system or grace. Jake's daughter swung her head as the door jingled and I entered. She worked her hands quickly and hurried to the place I sat, searching my face sharply with her eyes. She had a severe haircut, bangs cut so close to her hairline I could see her entire forehead reach all the way to her slender eyebrows. She began to speak harshly, asking where her dad was and why I wasn't still with him.

"This is why people should have cell-phones," I said absently, "I'd like a coffee with some espresso poured in."

"Careful with the bitterness, it might seep into your coffee," she replied.

She pushed a hand against the table, stood fully, and turned around to leave until she noticed Jake gliding in next to the espresso bar.

He said to me, "Don't fear being understood, my boy, somebody out there might be able to do more than just help." His daughter jumped from her corner of the room to join us.

He asked her, "Ellsie, what did I tell you Dostoyevsky said?"

Her eyes raced around her mind before she spoke, "'It is easier to lop off heads than to create ideas?'" He shook his head and she hurried with her next response, "He said, 'Sometimes you'll grab at a pre-existing thought pattern, thinking the current problem calls and demands for it, when really you need to come up with something completely new.'"

"Exactly." Jake turned to Victor, turning his question to him "So what do we do if someone forces us to do just that?"

His daughter looked baffled, "Nobody can force your thoughts and your actions are dictated by your thoughts so nobody can control what you do," she looked around hopefully, "right?"

"Well, everybody is trying to change one another, let's start by remembering that that doesn't work. You can never change another person. And if you're trying, something is messed up with you." He looked around the cafe, which was showing the shadows of a late morning.

"We don't have time for this," Ellsie said, her hard dark eyes trained on me under her translucent eyebrows.

Jake twirled his beard and spoke, "Victor, I want you to take over the cafe for a week, tops. Then you get the helicopter and find me," Victor laughed as he nodded, "I'm taking Ellsie and Ryan. Ryan, introduce yourself properly to my daughter before she argues about packing. Ellsie, you don't get to pack. Don't say a word about it. Ryan, I have your laptop bag."

Frustrated, Ellsie grabbed at the air above her head, "Ugh, Fine. Ryan, you better get used to being nicer to me."

"What have I done?"

"Nothing nice and it's upsetting," she said. She squinted her eyes menacingly at me and I couldn't tell if she was joking or not.

"To the car, both of you." Jake hugged Victor, as did Ellsie. I thought about my father, leaving him in his state felt just as bad as choosing to not look for my mother. I followed the pair out of the cafe and into the car.

We were driving the highway at about seventy. "I want the two of you to call every number with an asterisk next to the name in these three phones," he handed Ellsie a phone and two to me, "ask about the flying bird, if anyone's gotten wet, and where the badger is."

"Code words?" I asked him. He ballooned out his cheeks in thought then nodded. I got to the contact list of the first phone. The first people to answer their phones had no answers for my covert questions.

The third got my attention, "Ryan, isn't it? I recognize your voice. Yes, flying around, looking for badgers and other little wrong-doers. Tell the old man he has a place to stay here." The man on the line chuckled and the call was over, but I kept it close to my face, asking if he was still on the line.

"Who was that?" Jake asked as he twisted fingers in his beard. I told him the answers I had gotten.

"It says Simon. With an asterisk. Who knows him?" I asked as he growled from the front seat.

"He would have all the answers, wouldn't he?"

Ellsie chirped, "It's going to be okay."

His voice became darker as he drove, "Well, Ellsie, you got anything?"

"Nope."

"Ryan, you keep trying. This man isn't dangerous, he just . . ." Jake broke off.

Ellsie turned to me, eyes hollow, "He broke my dad's heart. Not once, not twice, but many times."

Jake said, "He should have had time to be sorry by now. Nothing to hold against him. If that's where we need to go, that's where we'll go."

"What do you know about my mom?"

I listened to his riddle of a response, "No knowledge within us is antecedent to experience."

"What?"

"You don't know until you find out."

"You stole that from Kant!" Ellsie shouted, laughing a bit giddily. "We won't know until we find out."

"That I did. We must base our knowledge on what we learn from experience. If not, it is not empirical but made with whims and instincts."

"I feel like that's what she did when she left the house last night," I said, "had an instinct."

"Or, for the first time in a long time, acted on an emotion."

"If she's such a strong detective, couldn't she have stopped them from murdering my cousins?" I felt a dryness in my mouth and my eyes welled up. I pressed my hand into my gut, releasing the pressure in my eyes and stopping the tears from running.

"Do you really want to assume?" He asked, "I think she had some sort of experience that led her to believe she could find this man. More than likely, she knew something we do not. What do we know?"

"I know that she was doing work with my father to find and capture a man that is trying to make a new kind of weapon, which this world does not need. He uses methods previously undisclosed to any industry because of their inhumane effects. She is, most likely, watching him. Oh, the inevitability of some inventions!" I thought of inventions, like the atomic bomb, and their inventors and how they coped with what had become of their work. I thought of Einstein on the beach and let my head fall into my hands.

Ellsie shared her thoughts, "Can't you modify your intuition with understanding? You said sometimes your intuition tries to modify what you understand, but can't it go both ways?"

"Suppose it can. Your approach to a problem must be receptive and immediate, that way you begin to comprehend instead of apprehend." I looked up to watch as Jake scanned the cars, flashed a hand to another driver, and created distance between the ones behind him.

"Isn't that what we're about to do, apprehend people?" I asked.

"Not after understanding fully."

"What if we don't?"

I saw tiny lines spike out of his neck as he flexed his jaw. A small dinging sound came from his pocket and he lifted his phone up to view it.

"Your dad sent me this URL, Ryan. Go to it, will you?" He handed me his phone and I studied the URL.

I opened up my laptop, turned on the internet-anywhere access, opened a browser, and found the page highly encrypted. "I won't be able to get on here if I ask politely," I said, as I opened up a program I had made that ate away the barriers. Within a few minutes, the site passed through and I spoke, "It's a page by the man my dad pointed out in the kitchen. He has information on my dad, but also both my parents' info and bios up here under the warning section. There's a few forums, one of them is." I started talking to myself, "Is it? Yeah, an anagram for the town we just came from and one for Oakland, interesting. Let's see," I continued to peruse the website, which elicited member support for a project just a few days before then and an upcoming one. "It looks like they're working on a project coming from Oakland in two days."

"Funny thing about this group, there are a few admins and a whole lot of members, but not a lot of average and reoccurring members, right?"

"Let me look. Looks like you're right. So," I searched the car with my eyes, "what do you think?"

"They're killing their own members, as well as children."

"And my father is seriously asking us to solve this?" I yelled from the backseat, exasperated at the untold atrocities we had at hand. I then realized I was out of my seatbelt and pushing against the seats to the front. "What can we do here, why isn't the government involved if we're dealing with child murderers and weapons distributors?"

Ellsie was pressed towards her own doorframe, expanding the distance away from me, "Sit down, will you? Why don't you think we can do this?"

"The technology they have would be of such a high value to your government and so little value to your citizens." At this moment, Jake's accent slipped into a smooth British one. "Mine as well."

"Have you been lying to everybody this whole time?"

"Not your family."

"Why, though?"

"We all have our secrets."

I shook my head angrily.

"There are entire companies built around producing these new technologies. The company is able to investigate their own equipment without a warrant or government involvement before they sell it to them. They chose to ask your father."

"At this point I'm not going to assume anything, but is this is the best investigation he can carry out?" I asked.

"We have metaphoric missiles to their handguns, Ryan. And we'll take theirs away." I noticed hesitation in voice as he added, "Or we'll simply find your mom after she has done that."

Ellsie turned and pushed at my chest, an undeniable strength against me, "Buckle up for the next million miles!"

Jake gave her an angry glare and said, "That's it, you're getting the backseat next time we stop," which I think helped me forgive him for carrying on a farce of an American accent. Jake turned up a Spanish dance radio station and we drove on until we stopped for gas.

At the gas station, I switched seats with Ellsie and we quietly waited for her father until I asked, "So what do you want to be when you get older, Ellsie?"

She said, from the backseat, "It is funny how no boy has been asked if he would rather get a degree or get married, isn't it?"

"What does that have to do with-"

She cut me off, "It means, you wouldn't understand if I told you, anyway."

"Ellsie, what did you see while I was in the gas station?" Jake asked as he got back in. He tossed a sandwich at me and two bananas at Ellsie.

"Two guys in karate uniforms getting into the front seats of an old cop station wagon. Weirdest thing I've seen all day." It was one of the weirder things I had heard of.

Jake smiled, put a few waters in the center console, "Guess we won't be taking a look at anything in this small town; they've got it covered. To the road!"

"How many more hours of driving, Jake?" I asked and looked back at Ellsie to see she had already eaten a full banana and peeled the second one.

"About three, maybe four, depending on conditions. You're lucky it isn't about to be a holiday, the roads would be packed."

Ellsie crossed her legs into a lotus position in the back seat, closed her eyes, and hummed, "I'll be back here, breathing."

I kicked my feet onto the dashboard and took out my laptop to look up information. I started with basic information about the drug my dad had found on my cousins. It had been created in a research lab twenty miles down the coast, patented as a research that had published findings on its ability to streamline workers as it satiated their need for sleep and food. Too much of it could kill, apparently, but that hadn't been published officially.

I put my laptop down, sighed, and rested my eyes as I said, "Why would they go out of their way to kill them?"

"They stole something that could only theoretically be used as a weapon; they had to test it on someone that didn't matter."

"I don't know how to admit that makes sense. It still doesn't. I have the same feeling I did when I saw the ways some boys slaughtered dozens of animals on our hunting trips at school. They didn't choose one or two, but went bestial and killed piles of animals. When I saw that these people hadn't killed just one or two people but all six of my cousins and hadn't let their bodies rest in their bed, I felt the same about them. They don't see that what they are doing is so blatantly inappropriate."

"You can hunt without filling every open grave in the cemetery."

I said, "But should you even be hunting people in the first place?"

"We are right now."

"Yeah, but that's different."

Jake's eyes pale eyes were pulling away from the road to look at me, "How did you deal with those boys back in boarding school?"

"Why do you ask?" This memory was a sensitive one that I didn't share often.

"Your mind's way of dealing is to look for a memory that easily can be adjusted and used as your mind's form of reasoning towards how the situation should be dealt with." I looked to him as he winked at me.

"Later that day one of them walked too close to me and I swung around, punched him in the face. When some of the others came to defend him, I knocked them out, too." I had never thought to pride myself on that, but I found myself grinning a bit too widely.

"Exemplary!" He said, "Not one of the best possible outcomes, but how you yourself attained it is exemplary." I looked at him nervously and he said, "Tell me stories?"

"You like to be entertained," I said. "I spend a lot of time in Oakland and when I'm there I see some ridiculous things." He chuckled again and the happy feelings the sound incited let me know that I liked making him laugh.

"Oh?" he asked.

"In the morning a few days ago I saw a woman peeing on the sidewalk as I was walking to the cafe. Another night, I saw a man walking on the sidewalk with one hand on his dick, the other on a crack pipe. Those kind of stories make me sad, but something in me feels like they're important to talk about. That place is in a state of emergency."

"Technically and figuratively." He leaned against the seat and the light from above the mountains in the distance made his beard glimmer as I looked at him. I realized I had a lot of questions for him.

"Tell me something, now."

"We thought everyone could be something when we were children. Maybe I'm in the wrong circles, maybe it's the times, or maybe it's just my perception, but everyone that is actually something doesn't get the respect they deserve and the nothings stand out and become popular."

I began, "I guess I'm naive. But, how do you know my parents?"

"Well, I noticed that they were very much somethings that pretended to be nothings for a very long time. Not easy to do. They disrespected the archetype that the general public likes to accept. And so I liked them, treated them the same way I'm treating you, and eventually they began to ask me for help. I never thought I could put my mind to use in such ways as your parents do theirs. Only when they came into my life did I begin to understand how everyone can all work together." His fingers perused the different notches and grooves on the wheel as his eyes studied what was beyond the wheel— or behind it in his mind, I didn't know.

"That is why I showed such concern. I don't know if we can do this, Ryan."

"Is that another test?"

"Might be."

"Well, I think we can, there's hope in the situation."

"As long as we have hope, you're right."

I shrugged and spoke, "My mom sounds like she's about to swing down and help us, anyway."

"Learn to rely on nothing you do not know," he said and aimed a half-smile that I returned as I was drumming my fingers against the doorframe.

A soft buzzing came from the backseat and we both looked up to see Ellsie looking for her phone. She smiled at us, "I can ignore you two for forever, but I'm not going to ignore my friends." She put the phone to her face and sang-spoke, "Ahoy hoy!"

I turned back to Jake and asked, "What did she just say?"

"Ahoy. Ahoy was first coined when the telephone was invented. It was the proper way to answer." He sighed, "She never does answer the phone the same way, though." He looked back at her. "I'm not as old as your dad thinks we are, but I do feel like I'm getting too old to chase after spies and scoundrels, let alone the whims of my own daughter."

"Spies and scoundrels. I think I'll update my account status as that," I jested at him.

"In case these scoundrels are already watching you, I would not do that." He chuckled lightly, making the situation he presented less distressing for me.

I turned up the mariachi band music. The light filtered in the car to fall on my face and I let it melt me as I grew exceedingly comfortable.

"Where are we going?" I hadn't fallen asleep, had I? The late night pacing the halls of my relatives' house had left me too tired to keep my eyes on the road. There was no necessity, though, so I decided to let myself go to sleep again. But I had already asked the question and Jake had already started answering.

"To Inspire Cafe's sister. Or would you like to be dropped off at your apartment? No, scratch that idea. That may be one of the worst ideas right now."

"Why do you say that?"

"I'm assuming that people have already stopped by and that it isn't safe for you, now. Simon is a smart guy, he knows everyone that walks into his cafe by name. If anyone new or suspicious is there or in his community, he knows."

"What's your story with him?" I rested my head against the window, yielding to a sleepiness that systematically overwhelmed my body parts.

"You don't really want to know." He chuckled then, laughing at what I did not know.

"Why not? There's nothing about it to be ashamed about."

"Because we're both men? No, it isn't because of that. I just like to keep my personal life close to the chest."

"Well, if you hurt him, that's not admonishable, either. That happens in life."

"It's not a part of my life I like to shed light on constantly."

"I've made my fair share of mistakes with the women I've been with. I would be ashamed if anybody I know now got to have a conversation with them."

"Ryan, I was a different person when I was with him. Very jealous and angry. I'm in more of an open-relationship with Victor now and I'm really happy."

"Really? Good for you."

"Not to say too much," he added, "but when I was with Ellsie's mother, I left her for Simon. It was a very big transition. But that is part of the beauty of human nature. We change, grow, and make new decisions."

"I won't remind you of your past too much," I said.

I let my lids close against my agitated eyes, slipping into sleep until a great time later when I had to blink my eyes against the glare coming from the white freeway.

Slowly noticing that this was a familiar area, I asked, "We're in Oakland, now?"

"Oh, yes," Jake said, layers of both annoyance and excitement were etched into his face, words, and body. His hands moved against the steering wheel like he was playing a piano and his eyes moved quickly from car to car to my face. I rubbed my face, almost slapping myself awake. We were passing most exits, which meant we were going to the Lower Bottoms of Oakland.

"I'll make my own judgements of him, just like I make my own judgement up about you." He looked at me speculatively and I continued without biting any part of my tongue, "You British bastard. Hiding behind a faked Californian accent," I said, letting my fingers trail against the windowpane as I did.

"Funny," he said in that clipped English tone, "most Californians don't notice that they have an accent specific to them, they think it's just particular words that only they use."

"Like dank," Ellsie said, "whatever that really means."

"I'm not from here," I reminded him, "I don't like that you thought you had to hide where you're from."

He shrugged and gripped the steering wheel tighter.

"Is it an immigration thing?"

He shrugged again.

"Well?"

Ellsie said, "Stop, Ryan."

Before silence could spread, I said, "Hey, are we going to Introvert?"

"You are a detective's son," Jake guffawed. "How did you know?"

I didn't want to feel placated like that, but I spoke anyway, "It's the only cafe in this entire area. It's a food desert here, so I can only assume."

"The only one?" Ellsie looked aghast.

"Well, we are indeed going there."

He took the Seventh Street exit and turned away from the industrious Cargo Street to a more suburban ghetto. Businesses long-since out of operation lined the left side of the street while the post office—the one that had displaced thousands of homeowners when it was built—sprawled itself out to the right, flanking the street and imposing on the sun.

There were probably ten semi-operational businesses in the Lower Bottoms, of these about six stood central to the cafe, a semi-safe place for everyone in the area to intentionally spend their time and money. Next to the cafe was a clothing shop with a giant shoe sitting on its roof and a tiny woman sitting at a sewing machine inside. Next to that was a bike shop that provided internships for at-risk youth and work-to-pay programs.

Spending money in an area that didn't have much of it meant that it would go back into that economy. Reinstating an economy was in everyone's hands. If I could have made the decision where to buy my car myself, it would have been in Oakland. Purchases like that reallocated resources and expanded the accessibility of them to people that needed them. I also liked the coffee.

Here in this tiny pocket of West Oakland, I happened to feel no judgement and no resistance when I showed my true colors. The entire neighborhood was like that. Nobody put a mask on that did not suit them. Nobody threw stones in their glass houses, but some people masturbated in them, disturbing as it was.

After reflecting on Introvert Cafe a moment, an epiphany arose in my mind, "Jake, I know the owner and his name isn't Simon, it's Tim! Something's wrong."

Jake's hands flared as he shouted, "Tim is not his real name. Tim is a close abbreviation to Simon. You should have picked up on that earlier. When did you first go to Introvert, Ryan? Very important to know. A coincidence is not something to look past."

I thought, "My dad sent me an email with just a picture of the front and the words: 'Go soon'." I chewed my lip while remembering, "So I went and met Tim—Simon, I guess—and some of the people that became my friends were there that day and I've been going every few days ever since. We're here." I thought a moment, "Does Simon know my dad, too?"

"Most likely, but if your absence from my knowledge is to tell us anything, it is that your parents have not told anyone everything." He smiled but it looked spent, forced, and sad. Some of his friends had kept secrets and now he had to spend time with two of their biggest ones, me and Simon. I followed behind him casually, but felt the unknown things stacking against my shoulders. We crossed the street, walking thirty feet under the BART train tracks to the cafe's door.

"Old friend!" Jake was yelling as he entered the place. Ellsie and I were so close to each other in his shadow, we were practically holding hands.

Simon replied almost immediately from his place in the cafe, "Good boy to return to your master!" His smile was wide. He removed himself from behind the cash register to stand at a reasonable place for Jake to hug him, but Jake instead leaned against the place where customers ordered. His smile was less large than Simon's, he almost looked pretentious, like coming to see him meant he could try to rectify past hurts.

"They used to love one another," Ellsie whispered into my ear.

"Do you get off on pointing out the obvious, Ellsie?" I knew it was a harsh joke, but the relationship between the two men was flooding me with anxiety.

"Hi, there, Ryan!" I turned to see Sol. Sol was a stocky Pacific Islander that was ready to take on anything because she had done it all. She had once volunteered for me to paint the cafe, could talk endlessly, and knew the meaning of community.

"Hey, how are you doing?"

"Well, well. There's this new proposed housing development and, because I'm on the committee, I've got to find some way to get it off the docket. Ripping up old communities for new ones, all over again!" I nodded slowly, letting her speak, "I know it would be a better idea to care about the people that already live here, not build for people to move here, but it is almost like nobody else thinks that way."

"It might bring more money into the area," I said.

"Huh, and take away jobs and culture, too."

"You don't know that that will happen."

"I've seen it happen, honey," she noticed the two strange faces eyeing me and smiled, "but you wouldn't know about that. Have a nice day." She pinched my elbow and slid away from me in the crowd and her booming voice once again erupted in a different conversation further away.

Simon walked over to Ellsie and me and smiled into her face. He then placed a big hand on her cream-blonde hair, tussling it only slightly, "We're always happy to see old friends," he said and turned to me quickly, "and new ones, of course."

Jake asked, "Would you like help closing shop?"

"It is an hour too early. Stick around and tell me of your new life. I'll make your drinks. Ellsie, what would you like?"

"Kave or matcha." She said both words, both unrecognizable to me.

Simon slipped a smile, "You spoil the child, Jake."

"She's used to working in a cafe of finer quality and variety than yours."

"Discrediting me already. It just so happens I have kava extract and matcha powder that has been shade dried from the tiniest, most nubile little green tea leaves. Be one moment. Ryan," he turned on his heel, "help me out?" I followed him into the back store room, past employee lockers and a bathroom, a place I had only hurried past in order to use the private toilet when the public ones were at capacity. Simon turned around when we had gotten past the back door and uttered, "What are you doing here with them?"

"I found out just today that my cousins were all killed with some inhalant that this guy, Leonard Kiljun, stole. Oh, yeah, my mother is missing. So my father asked Jake and me to basically find her and the Leonard guy. It sounds like he's been trying to get them but now that they made it personal, he can't deal. Do you know my parents?"

"I have to say, I do. Your mom got worried, wanted to know you were safe, et cetera. She had a right to worry though, these guys that work with Leonard Kiljun are all working out of this town and their greatest fears are few and far between—but your mom and dad are definitely on the list."

"So they threw me to a place right above them?" I asked.

"They were being a little selfish, setting your apartment up here. Don't worry about going back there," he began, but I cut him off.

"Yeah, Jake was worried, said I shouldn't."

"Don't you worry. Now, Jake shouldn't be here. We have a sensitive past."

"I can't convince you of anything, but know that apologizing is the best thing you can do. And don't just say sorry, get specific."

Simon wrinkled his nose, "I don't like it, but I'll do it." He grabbed a clear bag the size of my fist with powdery green contents and walked back to the bar. Ellsie and Jake were talking just as intently as Simon and I had been.

"Here is the matcha," he handed the bag off to Ellsie and picked out a tincture bottle from a low cabinet, "and here is the kava. Would you mind making some for everyone?" He handed off the bottle as she slipped off her barstool, went behind the bar, and placed a cup next to the hot water tower.

"Thank you, Simon," she said before starting.

"Now," Simon put his hands in front of Jake and began speaking, "I spent too much time thinking about how much I cared for you that I didn't think about how much you cared about me. For that, I'm sorry."

Slowly, Jake put Simon's hands in his. "What you said—I'll let it make everything okay."

Sitting and waiting for closing time made my mind restless. It began to dwell in the disquieting truth that children were dead. Knowing them and what I hoped they would be like when they were older and knowing that those things would never happen overshadowed the reality right in front of me. I had expected so many things and their deaths were not one of those things.

As I pondered, I looked up occasionally to see if any of my friends were stopping in the cafe. It was such a small community and so many kids that weren't making pocketfuls of money yet liked to live here, where rent was always cheaper than anywhere else.

Suddenly, unfolding before me in the door, was the girl that could help me conceptualize words like adoration. Cecilia. The girl that was helping me speak the language of love—even just to myself—and reminded me to feel the torturous pain of being lonely and in love. Being so close to someone so perfect made my body rush with happiness and guilt, all at once. My pores opened to breathe in her chemical makeup. My senses were abnormal and I was steadily losing my ability to keep a gap between our bodies.

"How was your night last night?" Her voice broke through the doubt I had created of not hearing it again. It was hard to press my own way through time and remember I had seen her only yesterday afternoon.

I began to tell her, "You won't belie—" before a soft substance smeared against my lips.

Touching my face with my hand, I saw white cream against the pale brown skin of my index finger.

"Try a latte that Simon made!" was yelled at me.

I ducked my face behind my sleeve, saying, "This was not made by Simon." I turned to Ellsie, "He consistently heats the milk well above one hundred and sixty degrees and this is tepid, though still fresh, meaning the maker was afraid to burn the milk and did not heat and froth it thoroughly." Her black eyes clung to her heavy lashes, forming an allegiance of aggression with her eyebrows, which were now spiked against me.

I turned my back to her, which conveniently placed me looking at another one of my friends as he entered. This guy was a bit of a buffoon. I heard him place a chocolate drink and sandwich order with Simon.

"What's the name for the order?" Simon asked.

"Bond," Tre said with a smile, "James Bond."

Simon raised his eyebrows and turned away, writing on the receipt and slipping it in front of another barista.

Tre gave me a look, hinting at something and walked over to us, "I was at home and trying to open a jar of pickles."

"Yeah," I said. "Is that all?"

"No, it slipped and shattered everywhere and I look at my aunt and go, 'Well we're in something of a pickle, now.' There was pickle juice, shards of broken glass, and floppy, vinegary cucumbers everywhere and we both just started laughing. I had to come here and tell someone."

Cecilia laughed and put her hand up to cover her smile, a gesture I was already familiar with.

Simon pushed half of Tre's order to him and looked to Cecilia and me, "Do not ever believe a person that talks about something so dumb. The least funny thing you can say and you go and say it, Tre!"

"It made me think, talking about liquids and all," Tre said, "that people say sexuality is a fluid, right?" His eyebrows wiggled and a smile grew as he spoke, "Does it freeze at zero degrees?" He laughed only to himself as we looked at him, wide-eyed and said, "Do you need to put it in a little container when you go on a flight?"

Before any kind of awkward silence could settle into the group, I turned and said, "Nice to see you, Cecilia."

I could see the sides of her eyes bunch up, "You too," she said quickly.

"How are you doing today?" Simon asked. His eyes flickered to the corner of the room where Jake sat. The pockets below his eyes deepened.

Cecilia lowered her head a bit towards her coffee. "Well," I could almost see her decision to tell a story forming into lines of words in her mind. She smiled, "I was walking down Peralta and was next to the school when I saw one boy all alone, almost sitting on the grass.

He was looking at something. He would raise his head to look up at the groups of kids behind him, making it seem like something he didn't want to share. It was something I needed to investigate. So, I went up to him, he was sitting right near the fence, and I saw that he had a mason jar in the ground and was looking at it intently.

"He told me that there were holes in the ground and he thought something was in them. I told him how I had found a snake in a hole like that on my playground when I was his age. More boys came over and the first one had me tell them about my snake and every boy had something to say about what they thought was in the holes and what they had seen before. When I left they were all sitting around the holes and mason jar, talking together."

Simon smiled at her, held her gaze for a half-second, then said, "You can always say so much while saying so little. I do like that." He looked behind him, "Oh, customers!" situated himself across from them at the register and said, "I'll see to you, now. Hello there, how are you?"

"It's odd," I said, "I think you're braver than me for being able to walk up to strangers, even children." My voice broke when I said the latter word and I felt a pressure on my eyes as I thought of my cousins.

"You are not ready for your own," she said as she slipped her small backpack past her glossy black hair.

"Would you like a walk home?" I asked uncertain if she would want to, but assuring myself that I wanted to be near her at this time of unease.

"Leaving already?" Came a complaint from a barista or friend of hers—I didn't know.

"Yes, I am," Cecilia said to her, then to me, "I would."

We walked towards the school she had passed earlier that day. The children were gone and a mist began to hang above the green of the grass on the other side of the tall chain link fence. Canadian geese congregated there at night and their yin and yang-shaped poops dotted the dewy field.

"How do you feel about yourself?" came my quivering voice from out of my own neck.

"I think I hate myself as much as I love myself," she said. "I hope that means I'm well balanced."

"Why would you hate any part of what makes up you?"

"The things that won't help me keep being me in the future. I have to motivate those things to leave or get better and I do that by hating them. Really understanding them for what they are."

"So you don't like to be inhibited by yourself."

"Yeah. Those little things that aren't competent, I don't like those things being inside me," she sighed.

"I have a problem envisioning myself overcoming myself." I saw an image of my father, with a tumor, in my mind's eye and winced as I spoke.

She looked to me fervently, "It could be because you don't love yourself."

I chuckled at the thought. "I don't know if I have enough feeling or emotion left in me. Sometimes I wonder if I'm a sociopath."

"You say that," she began. "Is it because you don't know what you feel or you're afraid of what you feel?"

I thought about the sides my mind took. It rationally argued against emotions and always won. Emotions were a burden on progressive action to me. "What are emotions based on?"

"Enjoying things or," she struggled for words, "not enjoying them."

"I can't always enjoy the simple things in life. What I do is break them down, analyze them, and try to figure out every detail about them." I looked at the skin on her cheek, at one moment orange from the streetlight above us, another moment, bluish white in the moonlight.

She laughed out loud and looked at me sternly, "You do not know my life, then. I cannot do that for anything that happens in my life. Nothing." She giggled the last few words but remained stern.

I hesitated, but spoke, "You can enjoy those things with analysis, too."

"It's not so easy when I'm around other people." At once, I was uncomfortable, worried I was pressuring her with my presence. "It's easy with you, though." She took my hand in hers. The cells in my body formed ranks, zoning in on every space in my hand that was making contact with her.

We wondered around the streets, soaking up the time we had together and almost completely unaware of what to do with it. We walked underneath wet, dripping trees and laughed at the things we had let slip from our mouths. I tried to touch her hands with my own but they found their old home in my pockets before I could. We laughed again, for no reason to remember. I followed her down the street I knew so well, a willing participant to her procession. We stopped walking and she touched my chin, tilting it up. I stopped breathing but couldn't stop moving until she plucked a jasmine flower and asked me to smell it.

"I'll make jasmine water and if I do it with healing intentions, it will help my aunt," she said as she carefully continued to pluck handfuls of flowers and put them into a grocery bag she had pulled out of a backpack pocket. I could see there was a process to it that she was following as she plucked the flower with one hand. To make use of the any possible time with her, I played with the sweet flower and brushed it under my nose, relaying the scent to my memory as one to do with her. As she explained away her aunt's sickness I saw probable reason for her to pass daylight hours away from home in a coffee shop.

"My family is of a different sort of time and place and they're," she said, as I had been guessing, "not easy to get to know."

"I know," I said.

"You think you do."

"No, I get it. Really. My family is an odd bunch, too."

"You say it so sadly."

"Bad things have been happening lately."

"Oh, we ward off bad things."

I was caught off-guard and cocked my head, saying, "Really?"

Her house was nestled between rows of other houses. The stucco and facade of the building were fully intact with no restoration, unlike most others in the Bay. A neat and orderly Victorian house was rare and I craned my neck to take its grandeur in. In her front yard, behind a nondescript chain link fence, a fire was burning. A gaunt and withered woman was fanning it.

Cecilia put her hand on my chest and looked at me with both lips parted. I wished she was kissing me goodnight, but she was not. She turned back around and rushed through the gate, yelling.

"Mama! What great thing are you doing?" Cecilia unslung her bicyclist bag and adjusted her outfit before stepping towards her mother's fire.

"Just burning the hair tonight, Cecelia." She was kneeling but put her hand up to her daughter's, grabbed it, and stood. I had the chance to see she was barefoot as she pressed her feet close to the fire, in a quick enough way that I would not know she had extinguished it if it hadn't immediately died upon her walking on it.

Her mother didn't spend long looking at Cecilia as she turned an eye on me, and said, "Your face looks as mine does when I have not been able to weep for my family. But now, as I say this, it changes to relief. You are happy, I know, but really, I do not know anything until you tell me." She took a breath in, slowly. A heartbeat's time to let me tell her. But how, when she was already so gracefully accepting of me, could I mar that good image with what I had seen? I had to look down, create movement on the ground with my shoe, and avoid telling her. She clucked her tongue, spoke succinctly to Cecilia in Spanish, and withdrew behind a door with squeaky hinges.

Cecilia made herself busy fluffing pillows on their screened in porch, rearranging small pieces of furniture, and then carrying her bag up to it. As she grabbed her belongings, she jutted her jaw towards the house and I followed her in. She shut the flapping magnetic curtains of the porch and opened a window inside the house that let us see a view of the cityscape, mostly San Francisco's. The twinkling lights closing in directly around us were only Oakland's. From this Western area of Oakland, we could see the juxtaposition of the sparkling and bright peninsula with two mighty bridges jutting from it, then around us to the eastern side a more plebeian view of meek orange lights.

Cecilia came out of the house and led me to a seat on the porch as her mother re-emerged. Without speaking the old woman went to the front yard, splashed a bowl of water over the ashes of the once-brilliant fire, followed by a bowl of leaves, then a plastic tote of dirt. All of the bowls she placed in the tote, which she heaved into the house before re-emerging, again. This time she held a towel, drying her hands as she beamed.

"I am Edna Maria Villery: shamanic practitioner, doula, Qi master, and healer." Cecilia sat by her mother with pride radiating to and from her.

Edna went on, "I offer thanks in advance to the directions, gods above and below, and mother of the earth." Wind with no verifiable source rose and fell. She put four rocks on the ground, thanking the four directions as she did. To the sky her hands raised and winds rushed up and down around us.

"Tell me what you have to do with the perfect bodies in the ground," she said sternly. I had not been forcing eye contact, nor she with me, but at this moment our gazes were fixed. Her eyes looked as if they had been closed for years before she tried to look at people in this way. I was only slightly aware that I was avoiding her question while beginning to journey down thoughts of my past. I wanted to hug Edna but I didn't want to displace the rocks she had set down. I did the only thing that made sense: I thought to her. I opened her up to the burial site of my cousins, the sorrow of my own aunt, the silly trifles of my own life, and then opened up still more until I felt my knees go out, my eyes lower, and everything was dark.

I was aware of Edna above me, but I felt alone until I heard Cecilia and smelled jasmine. She had reminded me of my youth before this current situation. Living outside of organization and institutions had left me missing the simplest things of a normal life, like a fresh kiss from a beautiful girl. That is what I dreamt I received as she put a flask to my lips. It was Cecilia, telling me I wasn't alone.

"I don't feel alone," I told her and she laughed brightly and my lucidity returned.

"You passed right out, I had to give you some liqueur to wake you up," she told me.

Aside from reviving me, the liqueur inspired my words, "Your mother needs to know my cousins were murdered and put in the ground." I heard her mother shriek as I continued to look at Cecilia. A few of her bouncy black curls were in-between her fingers, being entwined as she thought.

"Mama?" Her eyes glittered, "How many?"

"I'll tell you later. It's immaterial now."

"Six," I told her.

Cecilia's eyes welled with tears, "That many?"

I nodded.

Edna vociferated, "Let me tell you now that they were put there last night for a lot of bad reasons. Just like how I put my hair in the ground instead of in the trash, there is magic in it. There is magic being tried now."

I pulled myself away from looking at the women as I tried, once again, to understand the realities of the event. I fell short. I felt near-sighted. I felt debilitated.

Then Edna was again over me and I understood that she was hugging my head. I imagined her life to stop thinking about mine.

"Now my daughter tells people she is helping my sister when she finds me plants and herbs, but really, she is not. I have many clients, but no sick sister. She was murdered a long time ago and it hurt. Like your cousins being gone hurts now." She related it so well, I could not disguise my pain to her. I felt the warm trail of a pioneer tear on my cheek. More followed.

Edna said, "We will need reinforcements tonight," then brushed a feather across my shoulders, down my spine, around my head.

"Visitors?" Cecilia asked, "Tonight?" Edna smiled brusquely and she opened her mouth as a great animal call streamed out and she placed a branch woven in a circle on the four rocks. The wind blew again from the floor, up past me and into the night. Edna hooted the call again and removed four sparkling crystals from a tall shelf, placed them on Cecilia's lap, then placed a branch or root on mine. The room danced with her as her song echoed against its walls.

A chorus of hummingbirds flapped their synchronized songs behind our ears as they put the smells of their day's dipped plunder under our noses. She did not stop dancing but started yipping and cawing with the night's new noises. Chanting sprung up from her back garden as strange shadows glittered against the walls, pressing past furniture and faces to be seen as a procession of people. At once they looked very far away and at once they looked very large and close.

Cecilia pointed to a fuzzy orange image in the doorway, "Monks from the Hunan Province," she said,

"Very big ninja town, there. Why are they here?" Her whispers melted into the sounds of the room and the night and I didn't believe my voice was as strong as hers to be able to carry over all of those sounds.

I could see monks streaming out from it as they made a patronage through the house and out the front door. A group of them stayed and sat down in the screened-in porch. They did not rest into a meditative pose, but each of them remained seated on the balls of their feet with eyes wide open.

Edna was again very close to me, "They don't like for it to be even a little sacrificial," they all looked up, alarmed, "But I do." She said the words and I saw that Cecilia was now hugging a rattlesnake between her two index fingers.

Her mother strode past me, speaking,"With ease of abilities and manifestations alike, we will see them do well." A wine bottle was uncorked and it could have been a celebratory gathering if the snake hadn't been beheaded by Edna with a golden pair of delicate scissors. Cecilia drained the snake's blood into the wine. Edna and the monks did not drink. Cecilia smiled as she tried to get me to drink. Her eyes cherished mine and I allowed her to press the chalice of bloody wine to my mouth. After we had both had enough, Edna drained the glass, then delicately took a white ferret-looking creature out of it.

"That wasn't there before!" I yelled.

Edna said, "Thank you to all," then looked around. With that small gesture, she was telling us that the ceremony was over. They filed out between Cecilia and me. They took their time as they passed us. Each of them almost disappeared at a sprint in all directions once out the gate.

"Tuck your friend in, sweet child." Edna said as she kissed Cecilia and entered the house.

Nights in Oakland are never balmy except one night a year, when you want it most and the winds work for you. Tonight was that night, warmer than we were used to. We removed a few layers of clothing.

We faced the skyline and viewed my favorite city. Slowly, the excitement of the dusky ceremony wore on my lids and again I laid down to rest. Our faces watched one another speak for a few calm moments before she touched my chin and she kissed my skin, dragging her teeth to my earlobe and sucking behind them. I smiled as I returned the favor. It seemed we both fell asleep together.

In my dream I found a great and cavernous cave with the help of a hawk and the tiny ferret that had appeared in the cup. They led me to the back of a railway car, which I was used to seeing after so many weeks of using them. Through the railway car was a tunnel of darkness, then Introvert Cafe, then I was at the back of the cafe and in the cave, which had huge drawing of children under the ground, presumably buried. I stopped myself from panicking and called the hawk and ferret over to go back to the railway car, where I cuddled into them and finally stopped dreaming.

Chapter Three

Edna knew we had let our bodies rest against one another for the night and she woke us up with a severed chicken head. Sliding around on the plate she held, it ceaselessly played in my vision, inanimate but very mobile. Its blood pooled from the point where blade had made contact with fowl and the red trail looked like art as it danced and played away from the form it had once been confined to. The head itself was revolting in a way bloody plasma could never attain. My eyes closed before I could capture too much of the spectacle, but the image had an afterglow on the back of my lids that I couldn't dispel.

"Bless this before it is buried!" she then yelled something of similar length to Cecilia. Cecilia moaned in a way that had ceremony to it and I chanted like I had never heard myself chant. The red of the blood against the pure white of the feathers from the fowl was then taken away.

An aroma of sticky pink roses wafted in from the front garden. Our bodies pressed closer than ever before. An extra blanket was added and we let ourselves wait.

The dew lifted from the school yard's grass, the fog rolled above the neighborhood, and the nearby ring of the school bells marked the beginning of a day, and still our night lingered on. Edna became mother to me as she pushed chicken soup into my mouth and tucked and re-tucked blankets. Cecilia would not wake up and leave the newest bed in her home without me. She moaned this to me as her body stretched and warmed, so I found a stronger patch of sun and let myself melt like butter in it with her. Eagle feathers were swept over me, blankets tossed aside, and root altars put in their place, adorning any steady place on my body.

I finally arose with arms outstretched, picking up random objects that had been situated on me and placing them aside. I gathered Cecilia up by the bundle of blankets she had become, and looked around at the odd altars that had erupted around us. In an orange swathe of robe, the monk that had not left entered the screened-in room. Edna fed us the jasmine water she had made with what Cecilia had in her bag. We gulped at it, refreshed, and offered it to the young monk.

"He is their master," Edna explained, pointing to the monk, "and is now yours, too." He bowed in appreciation of the water.

"He is here," Cecilia said, "for you."

"Thank you, then." He nodded curtly. "Do you have a name?" I asked. He tucked his lips together and looked at me, completely composed and muted. Edna explained it away with a sweep of her hand and pointed to the center of the porch, where stones were placed in a bowl. She asked for each of us to select one stone in a high-handed voice and we turned on our heels as soon as we had. Edna kissed our foreheads and wordlessly walked out of the house. We let our feet create a harmonious rhythm on the street, clapping through silence, making a new beat.

Schoolyards had bees buzzing at the perimeters as the kids were playing in the trimmed grass with goose smatterings. The monk that had stayed followed us both and we were happy to point things out, hear how he spoke, and find out what he was like in our short trip the cafe.

The monk pointed to a trash can with Fresh Prince scrawled on it and asked, "What does that graffiti mean?"

To which I responded, "Fresh Prince? You've never heard about DJ Jazzy Jeff and the Fresh Prince?"

He smiled wide and said, "I like the sound of their names."

I shrugged and continued to ask, "Do you want to go by Fresh Prince?" He shook his head no and his nose crawled up his face as he made a face of repugnance, so I asked, "Then Jeff?"

"Yeah, Jeff." He said and I shrugged.

Cecilia opened her mouth, then closed it in a smile, "Jeff works," she said, stopping herself from saying anything else.

When our allies in the cafe turned to us, their eyebrows went up to see Jeff. I made a great sweeping gesture with my arms and said, "Presenting Jeff, the DJ from the Chinese region called the-" I looked at Cecilia and she nodded, so I said, "-the Hunan Province." I saw a curt nod from Jeff and he leaned over to me, smiling by my shoulder. He only stepped forward when I started walking toward the others.

I knew to tell Jake and Simon more, too, but they knew enough to join the entourage and not ask too many questions as we pushed past the line at the counter, disgruntling the already-aggravated barista, and plowed past the kitchen entrance and then walked past the back door that went to the empty lot outside. There, in the employee area and storage room, a fluttering Pacific Island fabric was haphazardly tacked to the wall, which Cecilia stepped up to and took down, coaxing the pins out. She revealed a crack in the white cement of the foundation, large enough and deep enough for us to all begin walking through in a single-file line.

We each had to crawl down, then quickly found a place for our feet and began walking haphazardly in the dark. Jake turned on a handheld flashlight behind me as I took the lead. We walked for at least a mile, surrounded by smeared black clay and sediment. Finally the path ascended dramatically. We looked around at one another and Jeff was the only one able to go up. He returned no more than five minutes after going up. He was smiling luminously like Edna had. He held two dogs and a white, oblong machine in his arms and was gripping them well for their size and the difficult descent.

"This is the place where they manufacture the sleeping gas, Artheum, isn't it?" I said, "That's his machine, isn't it?"

Jeff nodded and said, "Yes. What do you want to do with it?"

I nodded to him and he handed it to me. I gripped it in my hands, then turned away from everyone and threw it through the tunnel. It clattered, its plastic exterior breaking apart and the metal inside it lost pieces.

The heap of spare bits was disgusting to me and I looked back to Jeff.

He said, "This man you think about, I have seen up there. These dogs," he said, holding them higher so that their dirty leashes trailed against his bright orange garb, "You know them, Ryan?"

I nodded sheepishly as I put out a hand for them to sniff, "They are my aunt's."

Everybody seemed to be whispering or sighing when I said that and I looked down, a thick plume of phlegm erupted in my throat and I struggled to swallow. I choked on it and tears sprang to my eyes.

Jake said, "I'll take them for now, and return them to your aunt."

Everybody there nodded as some dense liquid dripped firmly near us, shaking us all from our reveries or deeper into them, I did not know.

Jeff recounted details to the group, "We will not go back the way we came, but go up in order to get out of her as fast as possible.

"That is, after we get the address here," Cecilia said and I nodded, faithful in her and yearning to stay by her.

Simon coughed, "I've had enough time to look through the area we're in now to know the area we're in above, there's no need to derail on an address."

"Then we leave," said Jeff with a nod. He back-tracked us a football field length away and both he and Jake pushed Cecilia and I up a drain. After we had hauled ourselves up another foot of piping we both saw a fragment of light leading to a full panel of it. We pulled ourselves towards it, out, and were on the street.

Jeff and Jake were close behind and we led ourselves southwest to the Lower Bottoms. After a few moments of camaraderie-born silence we started chatting.

"How did you know there were multiple exits?" I asked.

Jeff answered, "Your path did not see anything but what you needed to see. Mine saw differently."

Jake added while holding onto the dingy dog leashes, "There were so many more tunnels to go up other than that one. You, for whatever reason, knew to go there."

I took in my peripherals. "This is a really industrial part of town." The light of day was intimidating my eyes, but I noticed there were more warehouses, factories, and distribution centers here than in the Lower Bottoms.

"Better for making what kills kids," Jake said. Cecilia must have given him a nasty look because he added hastily, "Apparently. These people have now historically killed them without a second thought."

Jeff said, "Let us ponder what we are presently doing to misguide their path, then." He thumped a pocket on his shift and the white ferret popped out of it. "Your spirit guardian has come back to play," Jeff said as the creature gathered momentum away from us and down the street, the black tip of his tail bobbing recklessly as his body moved like a boat in choppy seas across the asphalt. He was so clean and neat as he ran down the dirty canals of filth and waste. I felt he would be much less clean the next time we were together. Jeff handed me a slip of paper with a smile. I looked down at it, then back at him.

"What are these numbers and letters?"

"What do you think they are?"

I guessed, "A password?"

Cecilia asked, "Where'd they come from, Jeff?"

"Maybe, your ferret got them for you."

"An ermine did that?" I asked speculatively pocketing the slip of paper.

"Ermine?" Cecilia asked.

"White ferret."

Cecilia bumped me with my shoulder, "You like the little guy."

"I'm not getting too attached. They get brown in hot weather. He's probably from China," I looked to Jeff as I finished my statement.

Jeff did not answer but began walking south. I thought speculatively until Cecilia took my hand in hers and my mind shifted and my thinking became intent on her hand and that alone.

Chapter Four

We made it back to the cafe in the time it would take to make a few shots of espresso. When we got there, we asked for drinks and the barista shook her black pigtails at us as she walked away. She spent her time making them, then wordlessly handed them to us.

Cecilia drew circles and then symbols on the table with her espresso while I drank mine. We let discussion about the crack that led to the factory go without having touched on it, maybe because we all knew we couldn't go back the way we came. There was something disquieting that had settled over us, a minatory astonishment that our proximity to danger had opened us up to.

Ellsie added herself to the group, saying good morning to us and her dad. She prodded us for words.

I asked, "What do you think's going to happen?"

"It's a proof by cases, in my opinion," she replied.

Cecilia asked hotly, "What do you mean?"

"Something's going to happen in either case."

I felt a nervous twitch in my face as I wondered what the categories of action were to Ellsie.

Jake was standing near her, grabbing her shoulder and I heard him mumble to her as he guided her away from us, "Don't be prey to the bifurcation fallacy."

Ellsie replied, "There's no third option and it's not like he can have this guy arrested without actually having him arrested…"

I couldn't hear what Ellsie finished by saying, but I heard Jake's loud laugh from across the room, "You don't know the people that Ryan is friends with, here! They have tricks!"

I watched curiously as I saw Ellsie look to Jake. Cecilia adjusted her beanie, which had been on, along with the rest of her ensemble, too long, which she told us in quick words. She withdrew to shower at her mother's.

"Does lunch, a good talk with all of y'all, then a siesta sound good?" she asked and we answered with head nods and high-fives. She bounced out of the cafe like a girl used to ripping through caves to find space vortexes first thing in the morning. The group encroached around me as I sat alone with Jeff and my coffee.

"She looks like the girl you slept next to last night," said Simon as he walked over.

Jake smiled wryly, "And you look like the man I want to—"

"Dad!" was whispered by Ellsie and discussion stopped for a moment until one of them lifted my bag from the behind the counter and placed it on the counter, along with a scone and light roast refill.

"Thanks," I mentioned.

"Did you hear about the credit card shutdown?" Simon asked us all with a jerking motion of his thumb to my computer.

"If they can do that-" I began to say more, but I thought to myself instead of speaking to them that there were definitely ways I could do something like that to Leonard Kiljun and his gang of weaponizers.

My computer booted up quickly and I was trying to make light move faster than matter. I was typing together chunks of code as I put it together in my head and looking up what I didn't know. I was on forums and search-sites, both old and new. Some helped me hack into databases where I really wasn't supposed to be, but was. Some helped me tune into what people were simply saying and doing all across the world.

It wasn't hard to become distracted. I didn't want to think too hard on what I was doing, or it would solidify in my head that we had indeed found the place where the people that killed my cousins liked to hang out.

I pushed myself to focus on what I didn't know enough about. When I did I found a myriad of well-intentioned forums about the shamanic practices being done around the world. What Edna had done was healing the harm done to me and my family. All of the past events were significant and the computer was helping me to walk the pathway toward the answer to my family's newest mystery.

I found new forums to begin a search of my parents on my childhood's last frontier. Their underground espionage professions were not in some fledgling stage available in public records. These two were not mere detectives, but major sleuths in communities not willing to tell much. There were "...well-coordinated, strategic, infrastructure re-allocations...." That could have easily been long-hand for demolition, that may or may not have been coordinated by them or a duo just like them.

There were cryptic and careful references that strained my patience.

"Whoever they are to the world," Simon said over my shoulder after some time, "they are on your side, as are we." He nibbled his own danish and helped me to more coffee.

"What we should get to know now is more about this guy, Leonard Kiljun"

Jake sniffed, "What your dad told us isn't enough?"

I ignored him and kept working, "His name is probably changed." I started typing it, along with some of the keywords I had picked up to find out more than that, and said after a moment's briefing, "We got all we need to know."

Simon and Jake exchanged heavy looks. I didn't think I knew it all, but I thought I was close. Now their pessimism was trying me. Jake said something to Simon that I couldn't hear and my anxieties asked me to go smoke with the street-kids in the back.

A bunch of loungers, the lot of them. Kids and child-like adults come into towns like these and loaf around to trash-talk school systems and each other in the same breath while rolling me one out of their tobacco packs. Some of them knew about cities, books, and teachings that intrigued me. Some of them had spent more time on the trains than I had and I liked to hear their stories. They let me listen.

"Have you heard about...." One of them began.

They were talking about the genius painter Katsushika Hokusai of a generation past. He was able to influence giants of his own time like Monet and Van Gogh and was currently known best for the print of a small boat next to a tidal wave.

I heard them say, "An economic downturn and an embargo on arts coming into Japan created a necessity for ingenuity, which made him produce the manga. Didn't he challenge another artist to a paint battle? It was a test of minimalistic strokes. To win he set a chicken loose on the canvas with some red paint on its feet?"

"Yeah, but with a big expanse of blue on it. There were a lot of street competitions between him and his confrères, but this one was to create a painting in the least amount of strokes possible. It ended when Hokusai placed a great swathe of blue against the page with a brush, dipped chicken's feet in red paint, and let it run across the page. He held up the piece and described it as some maple leaves floating on a river. How'd you know about that?"

"Went to art school. Learned about it," the other said. I had listened to enough of their tired voices to gauge more of them with the eye instead of the ear. I looked up to see two guys that were both wearing beanies like Cecilia wore often and patched-up denim jackets chatting near me. They had tight, frayed pants with grease and grime plastered on them and scuffed, vintage work books.

"School," groaned the other, offering few other words, but a look of disdain, instead.

"I'm still paying Fanny May for the loans, are you?"

"You know it."

"Working in the field now?"

"No—no way. You?"

"Same." I was just about to turn my back to them when I saw one begin rolling a cigarette and asked him for one. He wordlessly handed me the pack.

"You hear about this painter? He did that great tidal wave print with the small boat just under it?" Asked the art-school has-been of me as I handed the plastic package of tobacco back.

I heard him ask me but remained wordless before saying, "What were you saying about the chicken?"

"He dipped his brush in blue and set it on the paper to represent the river and," the guy licked the rollie's paper as he said it, "then dipped the chicken's feet in red and," and lit the cigarette, "set it on the paper."

A smile was playing on my lips as I said, "The ways that artists can use chickens is so extraordinary." I was thinking of Edna with the plate of chicken head, blood leaking rivers onto the plate's cracked finish. I thought of the headless spasmodic dance chickens do after their heads have been taken off. I saw a newly dead chicken dripping blood down its own body, leaking and splattering onto a canvas of blue, while still dancing. The dance of death itself is art. Even if it doesn't produce a two-toned canvas depiction, death is art.

The guys were still talking, but I was still thinking about the artist. The artist was able to see the lines of the world's connection. The shadows behind the form were apparent only to them. Chaplin's dance was an art, highlighting the shadows and ills of socialism to an uninformed public by entertaining them. The artist, able to fluidly pull one silky strand to affect an entire swath of web, saw the contradictions in our world and exposed them. The artist, whistling a hero's song and using all of nature to do what had to be done.

Without wanting to, I thought of the criminal passing off as an artist. Playing at pulling the right string of web as he engineered killing. He had to be leaking clues, I thought. I could find them. I could pull the web they were making apart.

I stabbed my butt in a tray and did not leave the patio the way I had come, but instead stepped to the furthest end and in to see Chloe, a radio DJ extraordinare, who was the only person I would trust to put her feelers out in just a particular way.

We greeted one another as she sat behind a sound-board, laptop, and a looping of chords and wires, a few of which hooked up to a couple of mics.

"Say a few things?" she asked me as she turned a microphone towards me.

I pushed the mic on as she faded out the song. I chatted about a few new bands that sounded like old bands and a few old bands more new bands should sound like, then signed off.

"Thanks for doing that." Chloe said to me after pushing the mic away, "My listeners like to know I have friends."

"Now that I've helped you," I said coyly, "would you help me?"

"You know that it wholly depends on what you need," she said with a set jaw.

"Could you put up a few ads for a found piece of equipment? Tell the owner that it was found and can be returned to them if they would like to meet me at the cafe tomorrow morning."

"You want it just on my show or all over?" she asked.

"As many places as you can afford. I'll pay back any cost to you." I said to her, looking her in her eyes. She pushed a few keyboard commands without looking down, then pushed up her eyes with a grin.

"Sweet deal," she said. "I'll do it for you. Consider it a way for you to donate this week to your good old Anarcho Radio Show." She smiled cheesily. I handed her the slip of paper in my pocket that had the equipment details and as I did all I could think about was that white ferret that had been helping me to get that information. The memory of him was fleeting, like smoke in a large dance hall.

I said, "I consider it done." She stuck her tongue out at me and I tapped her nose with my thumb. I called her a punk before leaving through the back entrance, onto the patio, then inside the cafe to pack up and leave with the crew for Cecilia and Edna's place.

Simon waved to us from the sidewalk while Jeff stood next to him. "I know Cecilia and Edna well; I've already been over to their house for some chicken dinners." He winked and continued, "I'll walk there with this guy." Jeff smiled and waved and Simon let his own hands push into his pockets as they walked east and away from the cafe. A guy washing the sidewalk from the nearby bike-shop waved at Simon, who nodded in response. My car was sitting outside the cafe and Jake stood next to the passenger door. I unlocked it and got in and Jake and I closed the car doors.

He spoke immediately, "I took the opportunity to go by your apartment. Destroyed. Somebody ransacked the place. I took the liberty of going into your rooms to see who may have done it."

"Somebody connected with this guy Leonard," I started to assume.

"The guy himself. I found a stub of a particular cigar from his hometown, which gave me no doubt in whom, exactly, we are dealing with." Jake began to open the door.

"Well, I have sent out a message to him and we should be meeting him shortly."

He nodded and held onto the doorframe as he said, "Good," before closing the door. I started the engine and felt comfort in the hum of it.

I knew the guy that operated the safe-guard car service on 7th Street and when I pulled up, he laughed, "Finally come to show off your nice car instead of just coming in on your own feet to say hi, huh?"

I nodded jovially and he took out two cigarettes and I waved mine away, instead taking out a few twenties and laying the spare keys in his hands. "You're ready to let me hold onto her too, huh? Well, thanks." He pocketed the bills, wrote a few things on the nearest clipboard, and continued to munching on his cigarette.

I set off for the shortest distance to Cecilia's house. From out of the Lowlands and into a different plane of existence. I wasn't convinced of anything working as I walked past the ghetto scenes of Oakland's Lower Bottoms. A woman shouted at a man as she slammed the car door on him. A crowd that was huddled on the ground around a game of pick-up-jacks inspired my soul until I saw money laid on the ground. Pigeons were dead in the gutters. An old, loud pimp yelled from the corner opposite of a liquor store. I was reminded of the time when one asked a girl I knew to work for him and told me I could gets legs for libido from him.

No, my pessimism was not increased by walking there, but I wasn't willing to drive my car around when the executioners were out to vandalize whatever they could of mine. The trick was going to be, I decided as I turned the corner of Cecilia's street, not to let her or anyone that I befriended to become property to vandalize.

Jake, Simon, Ellsie, and Edna were standing out on the front lawn, drinking lemonade and laughing.

Edna opened the gate for me and told me, "I once practiced Ayurvedic medicine on Simon's liver when he had cancer there, in his liver. He went through days of what you went through last night. Except I didn't let him leave to drink espresso like I let you do. Consider yourself lucky."

She winked at me as she showed me up the steps to the house and asked, "Would you help Cecilia in the backyard?" I nodded reassuringly and she pushed me past the front smoking patio, into the house, through the vast hallway, and through French doors to the backyard. I was just feeling as though a wind had moved us when I noticed Cecilia, in the backyard, which was a veritable Hanging Garden of Babylon. Greens and colorful flowers dangled from an intricate trellis suspended above the entire back rectangle of yard. This meant there was room for things like a chicken coop and other animal pens. Cecilia was next to the coop and was chasing down a chicken. By its appearance on one side, it looked to be a small, black-feathered chicken. Its other side was fully plucked and its naked pink skin shone as Cecilia gave chase to it.

"I'm usually very good at this!" she yelled to me. I watched her dive for it, unsuccessfully, once. It moved within my reach and I bent down, grasping it with a hand on its chest and a hand over its back. I held it in the crook of my arm. Where there were no feathers, my fingers touched the area hesitantly, then were intrigued and skimmed the surface of its skin. She drew close to both of us.

"It isn't as fun as it was when I first started chasing them down." She sighed, exasperated, "Back then it was a game, not a chore. Now, though, it's tough."

"I hope that's the only thing that gets less fun with time," I said, speaking from a deep recess of my mind.

She shattered my dreams, "You haven't heard? Everything is terrible once you do it enough times." I don't know how she thinks I looked at her, but I hoped there was something on my face to mask my pity.

"I'd love to show you just how terrific some things can be, no matter how often you do them," I told her, "but today hasn't allotted enough time to start that."

The chicken gave a rustle as Edna opened the French doors and gracefully took the bird. Cecilia's eyes watched her until she had left with the bird. She then turned her gaze to me. She opened her mouth, but the thought fell back in her throat.

Two orange fruit fell from a Jamaican passion flower vine hanging near us. A grey goat moved out of the shade and to a sunnier spot where the oval fruit now lay in its center. The goat bleated a call. Cecilia moved over to the animal and fruit. She picked one up as the goat looked at her, face smiling as she bit into the orange flesh and slurped the seeds and its orangey goop out. Cecilia gave the goat's head a pat and rubbed her palm into its forehead. She withdrew into the recesses of her garden and I followed her. To the back fence she went, passionfruit in her hand. Her legs found a bench to stretch onto under a great avalanche of cream bell flowers overhead. I sat on the mossy cobblestones on the ground next to it.

She pointed to the flowers, "Will you sleep with one of those Brugmansia underneath your pillow next time you sleep?"

"I will do whatever you ask me unless you ask me to love you," I said softly.

She looked away from me and to the flowers, "You might lose your mind," she said in a loud, singing voice, "or kill a man."

I tried to find her eyes, "All because of love?"

She laughed genuinely, "No, because of the flower." She turned from her view of the yellow flowers hanging against the blue backdrop of the sky to look at me.

"Not possible," I said, slowly placing my hand on hers.

She let her face slacken in confusion, then laughter erupted from her throat, "I think you should come out with me tonight. I'll show you a bit of my world before you think you know it all." She turned again towards the sky and I felt free to furrow my brow. What needed to happen was not necessarily that Cecilia and I saw too much of each other's vulnerable sides.

"When we have less to stress about, I see us being able to do that." I looked at her to gauge her reaction, but her face remained placid. The daylight's dapple lighting played on her face.

"I've done what you're doing before," she said as she turned to look at me. "I've abstained and tried to ignore the way my body feels magnetic to another person. I've not done a thing because it wasn't good timing. But it didn't work. I stopped my stars from aligning by doing that."

I faced her, "You can't be saying—"

She cut me off, "I am."

I stood up and she followed suit by standing up on the bench. She bent over, drawing herself closer to my face with hers, then her lips were brushing my neck as she whispered Spanish words quickly in my ear, then bit it. Putting her hands on my hips, she turned my body with her hands towards her house, jumped lightly from the bench, and started a slow walk past goats and chickens to her house.

As she passed me, she said, "You both disappoint and overwhelm me," with a vulnerable bitterness, like dark chocolate that will not tolerate being sweetened to placate imperfect palettes. I did not want to watch her added to, nor subtracted from, by any person or thing. I wanted to watch her melt in the sun and re-solidify in a casting of herself, not me. Not her mother. Not the man killing my family, or any of the people helping us. I just wanted her to be her. If I were to do that, I would have to accept her word as my law.

I jogged a few paces up to her, reminding myself of her earlier words, "I'll let your stars align, but I won't let you put yourself in harm's way."

I stood close, almost grabbing her, but my hands hesitated above her, "Don't let this, anything, or anyone change you, Cecilia."

She touched my chin lightly and she said, "I couldn't change you if I tried, Ryan, but you may choose to change. I can see myself doing the same for you."

"Do you know me better than I think you do?" I asked her this as her hand traveled up my jaw and into my hair. She smiled and nodded. Her thumb rested against my temple and her fingers massaged around it. I let my hands fall on her hips and turned her body towards her house, as she had done to me just earlier. I meant to push her gently towards the house, remind her of the chicken we were going to kill, take both of our minds off of what we were planning, but in my moment of hesitation her hips had turned to press against mine.

"If I am not allowed to change," she smiled as she pushed my body against her fence, which had the same overgrowth of vines as the roof of the garden, "I am going to show you what I like to do."

I gripped for a place to hold onto but the green vines were supple and broke. I looked furtively towards the house, grateful that there was no view of the two of us from it. I willed myself not to do what I wanted to do. Cecilia was holding me by the wrists gingerly, strength broadcasting from her eyes. She would have me, she was saying with them.

"How did you feel when you first met me?" she asked.

"Magnetized," I said. I wanted to be more honest, I wanted to tell her about my respect for her, for what I had seen her accomplish, how I was so happy that our friendship had begun and was taking us here, but her mouth was next to my ear, breathing heavily as she took off our clothes.

At that moment, a great bellowous chanting began from inside the house. I looked at us together to see two puzzle pieces needing to meet. Whistles and bird calls came from the group inside. Cecilia's face breathed in the smells from my chest, then my navel. She touched the inner parts of herself to me, first gently then with a deep hunger and want. I noticed a wind sweep against the curtains of the house, creating a clamor as it knocked objects together, then rustled the plants throughout the hanging garden. She touched the inner parts of herself to me, again and deeper. Singing came from the house and bird calls erupted from all over. Our bodies separated before I pulled her up. She pushed me into the green roping vines and we let them cushion our movement and hold us as we held one another.

As I put my clothes back on, she picked the cream flower from above the bench and brought it to go under my head as we consumed a siesta together.

I pulled a dream together in which I was standing in a low valley of ice, with the hawk and a crow fighting above me. I chose a part of the ice to walk towards before seeing a cave in the ice. I touched the side of it as I went in, noticing no cold or sharpness from the rocks.

I walked along the cave for a long time before seeing a bullfrog sitting atop a stick. He lifted his arm and told me to continue with freedom. I could walk along the plane of the gone if I did not accept hindrance. I moved further until there was a fissure into a large expanse of rock that looked over a long mountain range. A wind swept around me and the senses of comfort and ease was enormous. I looked around to see if my friends and family would come. I only saw the hawk, which was descending from the sky to me. It landed on my arm, shuffling its feathers a few times, then stiffened as a wind swept down from the clouds, through us, and into the mountain range. I watched as it displaced snow like wind shakes trees at lower altitudes.

"I would like for my cousins to be here," I told the hawk.

He nodded, "Bringing them here is one of your missions, Hero."

"So that is what is happening," I said to him, "I am being asked to be the hero."

"It is true spirit counselors have asked for you if you are the hero of this time," the hawk spoke, "but nobody has asked you if you will be because you must be."

I sighed, and thought about the dream thus far, and said to the hawk, "I have more to ask you, don't let the dream end." He jumped off of my arm and began both flapping and becoming invisible at the same time.

"Talking like that makes it difficult," he said before returning to land on my arm. I stop thinking about this as a dream but more of a real experience before he spoke again, "The mountain is not what will make you trip, but the small pebbles in your path." I walked on the great rock with the hawk as I looked towards the mountains before me. Purple rocks on every mountain jutted from beneath a white snow drift or blue layers of ice. For miles one color receded into another. I could imagine my cousins there, but before I did, the hawk shifted his talons on my arm.

"They can go higher," he says as one of his wings points to the clouds. Without hesitation I willed us to be there. Like the mountains below, violets and blues were interlacing on the white clouds we were now on. I could see the hawk's chest expand and recede as he breathed in meditatively.

I followed his lead and meditated on my breath before saying: "I thank the four directions and each person standing at the winds, the god above, and the one below, in advance for letting my family come to this place." I heard the hawk far away from me screeching as I opened my eyes to see him flying into the sun, which had not been above the clouds before I had closed my eyes.

The bullfrog was, again, sitting before me and said, "Help others, like the man who put the children in purgatory, to find this place while still alive, and you will find no obstacles in your path." I nodded to him and he nodded back to me.

I climbed down out of the clouds and saw Cecilia's face inside of the dark tunnel. I was falling down. She was concerned and her black hair was flying in my face, making her harder to see. It was her name I tried to yell several times before drum beats pushed my boundaries of awareness. I heard them and was no longer falling, no longer near Cecilia's trembling face, but hearing so distinctly the rhythm of shakers and drums. Half in the whiteness of the dream, half in the darkness of reality, I started to stand on two shaky legs.

Waiting for me was a band of my patriots in the dim evening light, each sitting before me, under the hanging vines, as they tapped and shook their instruments. I rejoiced in my own happiness to see them. I felt victorious just to see this newly forming family.

"We take second place to the bandits, remember," said Edna sternly, reading my mind.

Cecilia was holding my back and hand with both of hers, asking what had been in my dreams.

"Heaven," I said, without thinking it was altogether the right word, "I can take my family there." She looked at me oddly and I said, "I can take my cousins, but I need to cure this man Leonard first." I sat up with Cecilia's help, inspiring me to tell them, "With your help, tomorrow, I will. The cafe should be cleared of all but him and us."

Jake was looking at me aghast, "You must be insane or dumb. Your parents would be doing this so much differently. Better. They would be sending him to jail, not to-" he looked at Edna.

She raised her hands, "The boy did say heaven."

Ellsie put a concerned hand on him, "Dad, you're going against what you told me that thought is abstract, the—"

Jake stopped her, "Exactly, so if almost every culture has thought there was a god, heaven, et cetera, then they are all limited in thinking that. As are you," he pointed at me as he spoke.

"No, Dad, you're limited in thinking that you can know everything. You can't and you know it," she said while tugging on the beads on her drum and moving it further from her dad.

Edna spoke, "Jake, I was sensing a strong desire of yours to leave."

He shook his head, "No, no. I'm here for whatever you need. This is your town, not mine. Don't let me redefine what you think is best."

"Good," Edna said with a smile. "Then that was before but it is gone now. Would you like to stay for chicken dinner?" He nodded earnestly and took his daughter's hand in his to squeeze it lightly. Edna spoke again, "I would love the opportunity to explain some things with you."

He looked humbled, "I think I have some opinions and assumptions that are blocking my sensitivities to what it is you're able to do." Edna smiled and took him inside with Ellsie and Jake at their heels.

Cecilia and I embraced. Her chin rested on me comfortably for two moments before she asked "No nightmares?"

I laughed off the question while looking at her with utmost transparency, "None."

She nearly jumped with excitement when saying, "Then I'll make you a tea of that flower and kill a chicken in your honor so that you will have visions."

"Cecilia!" I almost asked her just by saying her name, "No slaughtered chicken is necessary."

"Really?" She said keenly, "The slaughter is my least favorite part. I cannot change Mama but I will not gore at the ceremony, for you."

"Sweet girl." I said, "Help me to some beans and rice?"

Her laughter sounded like chimes, "Sounds like you want a burritos sans pollo."

"Actually, I do."

She led me back inside. "Why not go out?" she asked.

Now that I had seen the spirit plane, I was in even less of a rush to see anyone I knew go there. Going outside didn't always mean putting everyone in danger, but when there was a gang leader I was baiting to find me, it was a better idea to stay cooped up.

I told her, "You stay here. Hold down the fort. Jake or Simon can storm the castle walls for burritos while Jake theorizes about heaven."

I laughed but Cecilia put a hand on my arm, "Will you explain? Did you see god? Lights? Colors?"

"Certain colors..." I began before trailing off until my eyes met hers and they pried more words from my mouth, "I was under the impression that every person has god and heaven in them. I'm nothing special for going up there, everyone can with the right direction- your mom's direction helped. Every idea anyone has ever had of those two things has been real because it was within them. The individual makes it real, not god and heaven making the individual."

"You have the entire universe within you." Cecilia put an emphasis on saying it was me, "All of creation. That is how the monks came."

"What?" I was startled, "They weren't just staying with you?"

"No, they weren't," she said. "They were within you and came out last night. Like magic," her lips played with a smile as it moved like a jumping rope between her cheeks.

"That is the idea I got in the dream," I began, "but not how I feel within reality. Everything is contained within every person, you just have to ask for it to become."

"You seem to think just anyone can become," she smirked at me after speaking.

"My cousins would be able to," I told her as I played with a vine.

"Because you ask them to 'become'?"

"Don't defend against any assumptions, Cecilia." I tilted my head at her.

"Don't make me defend myself against you," she put a hand on my shoulder, then removed it quickly, and added, "Hero."

I warned her jovially, "You call me that again and I'll catch you like a hawk catches a crow!" and gave chase to her. She ran and cawed out like a crow caws as the memory of the hawk on my arm came back to me.

She opened the French doors and ran inside. My breath caught as I looked down to see a hawk's feather sitting on the doorstep. I picked it up and walked in.

"I do not eat the sacrificial ones, nor does anyone," Edna said when I was entering. She stood preparing a fully plucked chicken, continuing to speak, "I take apart its entire body and bury it with either somebody seeking treatment or alone, by myself." As I placed the feather in a vase near her window she gasped, "Is that Wakken Tanken speaking to you?"

I asked, "Who?"

"Oh, it is!" I twisted the base of the feather in my fingertips. She put down her work and continued to gasp, "You are blessed! You are!" She then opened a jar next to the chicken and scooped the liquid into both hands, letting the blood gush out and around my head and shoulders. I blinked open my eyes after it had drained past my forehead and temple. It dripped from my chin down and I gasped towards her. Cecilia opened a drawer and took out a washcloth, patting it against my face, down my neck, and across my chest and shoulders. She finished with a smile and dabbed my face and nose.

"I have the spirit on my side," she said, "so I know better than to put you through Ayurvedic treatment." Edna kissed my forehead and turned her head to kiss my Adam's apple, or trachea, "Spirits know when one is completely pure enough to be a blessed one."

Thoughts of what her daughter had me do, the seduction in her garden came to my mind.

She twitched, "Ay, I'm still telepathic, you know. Very sensitive in this mind here," she tapped her hand to her head and then began to light a sage stick with a match. I thanked all six directions inwardly.

Edna looked up to me. "You know the six directions, now. How?"

"I dreamt them," I said placidly.

"You did, eh." She turned over some food on a pan while holding her hip with the other hand, "I'll include them in ceremony, but there is no ceremony tonight. Tonight, we all eat dinner together here. Cecilia, you set the table."

"Jeff," I asked, "were you there when I woke up?"

"No," he said, "I was on your plane, protecting you against the dragons." I faltered in thought and realized I had not seen any dragons.

"Exactly," he said without a smile. "Your safe return will forever be protected."

"Thanks Jeff," I heard myself catching on his name. "Do you mind me calling you that? It feels amoral to use a misnomer on one of my friends."

He held my gaze and spoke, "I have no need for representation on this plane. If I am represented, or misrepresented with a silly moniker, I am still one and contented."

"Representation is how meaning is depicted," I said.

"He is meaningful enough," Edna said as she pushed herself out of the kitchen with half a dozen dishes layered on her hands and forearms. The dishes were making every ethereal noise possible as they popped, sizzled, and cracked as they cooled. She smiled, freely joyous as she came back into the kitchen.

Jeff continued in a different tone, "There is an ancient story that I have learned from." His young eyes grew heavy-lidded as he began, "It is about an emperor who went out hunting on horseback with his falcon. When he came upon a stream, he knelt down to drink. When he did so, his falcon tore from the sky to knock the cup out of his hands. When he tried again to drink, his once-tamed animal was acting on some bestial instinct, knocking it from his hands."

He shook his head and looked over at the window. He then continued, "Only after turning on the hawk and killing it was he able to drink from his cup. After he did, he become very ill." His story was not over, but windows had slammed open, knocking the feather from the vase on the sill. It landed between our feet, squarely on the oakwood floor. I compared the intricate wrapping of clothe around Jeff's feet to my minimal converse, which didn't protect against the chill that was entering the room as I watched the feather move with the wind.

He picked the feather up off of the floor and tied it between the wooden beads around his neck as he spoke, "Many paces up the river was a poisonous snake, leaking its venom as it died into the stream." I realized how the story had come together, how the falcon was protecting his master and how the emperor became irate before thinking.

"I would like to be your falcon to prevent you from being either hunter or killer while you seek retribution." He told me, "You are to cure and of this I can sense you are aware." He finished speaking in an exuberant way, "But, you'll need help before it's done."

I thought of a turn-of-phrase, "What doesn't kill me might kill you, though."

He said seriously, "What does kill you will kill me," He smiled at me and I smiled back, both of us shaking our heads at one another at the incidental pressure we had placed.

I rubbed the top of his back, "Let's get you some dinner." He nodded and moved into the dining room, an extremely over-furnished room with an ornamental ancient grandfather clock adorning the end of it, flanked by two windows with views of twinkling lights on the bay. Edna smiled as we entered, as any hostess does when she sees the last remaining guests enter.

"No burritos necessary!" Cecilia joked as we had all finally sat down, "Mamacita went all-out! Shall we start with the figs?" She opened a pot with raw purple-skinned, pink-centered figs that had chicken livers sitting like cherries above them.

"Glazed with a cinnamon, pine nut, and gooseberry chutney," Edna added.

"Some rhubarb, raspberry, and pomegranate tarts that I had to make completely," Edna opened the lid of a dozen pink tarts,"To be eaten before, not after, with sweets."

Cecilia opened two more dishes and steam erupted from both.

Edna looked lovingly at the soups, "Bone broth with broccoli, acorn squash, mushrooms, and asparagus. That one there is completely vegetarian lentil, carrot, cauliflower, endives—you get the idea. Steamed spinach with loads of ghee and garlic," she sat down and opened a pot at the same time a wind blew the butter aroma around the room. We all exhaled the fragrance towards the table's center and smiled.

"Then some good grains like muesli and barley cooked with kale and collards to put below this chicken." She sat down and began serving. We followed her lead and sat down, getting to know our silverware and the plates we were about to fill as we did so. My exhaustion overwhelmed me as I sat down and Cecilia helped me to put a plethora of food on my plate.

"Omit the chicken eyes," I said to her, sternly. Cecilia batted her own eyes but dropped an eye from the ladle it had been dangling on.

Edna put a hand to her mouth and continuing to eat as she looked directly at me, across me at the other head of the table. Her fork stabbed an eyeball rolling on her plate and she promptly put it in her mouth and swallowed.

"It prevents harmful things from entering you if you eat it." Cecilia rolled two in front of me.

"Let me first whet my appetite," I said idly as I added a few pieces of other food to my fork. I realized I was procrastinating eating the eyeball and, without thinking, I speared one solitary eye and swallowed that mass before taking in the second.

Some at the table went up in a jeer or low murmurs at the small affair. I had to smile and laugh as I finished pushing the food toward digestion. I ate the second to simply remove it from my vision.

Jake asked Simon, "So, I never asked how it is having a business here."

Simon said, "This area has few small businesses. Few cafes. That makes us target to three things: business, crime, and lawsuits. Does the good money outweigh the bad losses? For me, yes, but only because of the community." Simon sighed heavily and looked at his untouched food. "I gripe no more and am only grateful," he took a bite, "for abundance!"

The table cheered again. Everybody, including Ellsie, ate. She sat next to Angelique and Edna, to whom she looked frequently and then asked "Can I shadow you tonight?"

"You know what I do is great and powerful," Edna said and Ellsie nodded. "Good intentions are important but not always enough." The whole table seemed to be listening. Ellsie and Edna seemed to be listening to one another with their eyes before breaking their mutual gazes and reforming their faces to smiles, scooping steaming piles of vegetables onto their plates and looking around the table.

"You have a strong girl, Jake."

"In all respects. Her mind is as sharp as her knuckles." Ellsie looked at her father meaningfully. "She disapproves of violence."

"As do I. Promoting thought is better than demoting it," Edna said fluidly as Jake nodded.

"Consider your opinions considered by me." He laughed as he squeezed the words out and the pink tarts into his mouth.

I laughed, too, as Cecilia had squeezed my leg with her hand. I laid my hand on her wrist under the table. Looking down at our hands, I saw her black curls sweeping towards the teal tablecloth, a shining black sky against the babbling river under it.

Without looking, I leaned in to smell the jasmine scent of her hair and whispered, "A master painter must have made you."

She pushed my mouth aside with her cheek and whispered to me, "How can I eat what is on my plate when you, too, are in front of me?" My leg shook softly under our hands and her fingers slid from under my hand to grasp my thigh tighter.

Edna said to the table, "Let us not forget ceremony," and lifted a snake from under the table.

I looked to Cecilia, saying, "I thought she said there would be no ceremony."

"This barely cuts it," she said.

I looked back to Edna as she pushed the snake's fangs into a tiny jar with clothe over the top and then, holding it by the head to her plate, she pulled a butcher knife from the table, above her head, and then down on the snake. My blood was so confused, it didn't know if it should stay in my groin or rise to my brain. Regardless, I felt like there wasn't a drop of blood in my own body, anymore.

Behind the snake's flared head, blood spurted and she then lifted its body to drain its blood into the wine in her glass. She held it up like you might hold a garden hose to stop the stream as she passed it to Simon, then Cecilia, who drained some blood into her glass then passed it to me.

I shook my head, no.

Edna nodded hers, yes.

I shook my head again and Cecilia drained some of the snake blood into my glass.

"I thank every heavenly body, in advance," she said, "for the guidance they bring."

Then Jake and Ellsie took some before handing it to Edna. A tiny jar, which I knew was holding the snake's venom, appeared in her hands. The winds in the room unsettled the tapestries as she put some in her mouth, lifting the bloody wine to her lips as well, then swallowed.

She looked to me and threw the small clear jar, which hung suspended in the air for a moment while I decided to catch it. Then, when I had decided, it fell to my hands like a ball in a hoop. I uncapped it and put two drops of the venom on the underside of my tongue. I swallowed my mouthful.

We made mutual eye contact and I saw our two bonds, intertwined throughout time, stretch out in front of my. Like circles or soap bubbles, our paths had crossed before in various ways.

I sought our first contact, in the days preluding Zarathustra, before any monotheism existed. I asked Edna about Zarathustra and she told me and I absorbed story of a time 18 centuries before Christ when the first god came to earth to Zarathustra, who was the first human to believe in heaven and judgement or a hell to contrast it. Though the god that came through Christianity was real, so was this one—it was as real as Zarathustra, as Brahman, and Krishna. As real as their creators because their creators were aligned with their eternal soul. When one remains devoted to the godliness they possess within their soul, they are able to find a loophole in the cycle of death and birth. They are one with God. Some choose a life in between two planes to help those on earth find this and ascend. Edna and I had reached a full understanding in one of these contexts.

She pushed the energy that we had made while speaking telepathically into the earth and to the table, and said," Let us go into a new direction. Start by thanking the reasons behind day and night, the four directions, the earth, sky, and the seasons individual powers you should know I wish for this to be and I offer thanks in advance for success."

When we opened our eyes, Edna said to the table, "We have just explored and should remember a Hindu lesson. The Mahabharata states: 'What is found herein may also be found in other sources. What is not found herein does not matter.' Remember what the spirit needs and nothing else." The curtains flew open to present a view of streets beyond ours as we raised our glasses and finished what was on our plates.

"To ask you to be there tomorrow means a great deal to me and I would like to ask you all again to be there," I said. They all nodded to me in salute. I looked to Jeff, with what he shared with me; Jake, with his love for his family; Ellsie, for her love of logic; Cecilia, for the love she had for life; and Edna, for her love of her religion. "Thank you all, I love you." I sat down and they all inhaled to cheer and smile again, but I pulled the breath out of their lungs and back in. The wind in the room began to circulate and, without any more precedent, we all began to breathe deeply and meditate.

Only Edna peeped open an eye when my small ferret came into the room and, with a little hop, found a place on my lap, where it placed a note that it had untied from a back leg. I realized where the information I had given for Chloe's radio announcement had come from, that I would use this note when I needed it more than I did now, and that I had a responsibility to the group to meditate with them.

I breathed in visions of the heavenly plane I had found earlier as a stable place that I wanted this group of friends to feel and touch. I heard Ellsie singing a song that was full of breath and rhythm. Cecilia sang as a siren, toning to Elsie's chant. They were singing of duality. A yin and yang force created by another godly being from a different time, but the same space. I breathed out frustrations and let the knots unwind inside me. I breathed in the deep violets and blues my mind had made mountains out of. I heard the girls singing with Jeff now as he let loose prayer chants. Edna whistled to us all as Simon and Jake linked up deep hums. The dinner party slipped into their own comforting heaven.

I could rise above the table and touch each person's vision. As I took a moment with each one, they talked to me as the eternal souls that they were. Our paths expanded both behind and in front of us all in an instant. Edna whistled to us again and we all lifted higher above heaven to where the hawk had flown. I smiled as I felt Jeff himself take us there on his wings, across the table. We saw a pure, unadulterated white light. Each person was given a path in that instant, and then told about the accessibility of this plane to them. Like a good meal with friends, they were able to enter with leisure and grace. Then we were back in the dining room, all smiles and bright eyes toward each other.

We washed our plates amicably together and retired to the porch, where we watched the sun clock in after a long day's work.

"We can still appreciate this world," Simon breathed out.

Edna answered, "It is on being righteous while in this world that our attention must be. If you can practice meditation while watching the sun set against the ocean, you are close to righteous. If you can go to sleep and rise and still be practicing waking meditation throughout life, you are on the right path."

We were all still absorbing Edna's words and absorbing our own analysis of the collective experience we had just had. Cigarettes burned and Cecilia's thighs rubbed against me and made a wild lion ask for something from both of us, which I did not speak about or act on. She kissed me on the ear and went to her room while I finished a glass of jasmine water. Jake and Simon's past relationship flamed as wine flushed to their faces and questions about a room upstairs, for them, to share, were raised. Cecilia came down with a white hoodie jacket for me, which she said reflected my purity.

Edna flickered her eyes at the objects and through her I saw her fear that there would be blood. Red blood on white was not abnormal to her, I thought as images of the chicken's bloody, severed head raced back into my vision. Headless, the bloody chicken wobbled in front of us. I thought, instead, of my own blood staying inside my own black body and felt safer, more secure in that. I donned the hoodie underneath my jacket, willing that I wouldn't need to loose any blood or strength. I said goodnight to Edna and Ellsie as they filed inside the house, complaining of the cold.

I rested on the porch's new bed with Cecilia. We thought out lines and whispered them, "To your body I so much care; I have writ you a prayer," and, "into you I will dive; in springs there I'll thrive." Our toes curled around one another and we looked to the full moon as we made up our sweet words to one another, inspired by everything but sleep. We twisted and coddled one another with our own bodies and hands.

After uninterrupted jubilation, she cocked her head and said, in a distraught way, " Companionship comes to me like water from hole in a boat. At first, it is quite unexpected, then, slowly it fills my entire vessel and I am forced to become part of its entirety."

"Becoming part of the sea doesn't sound so bad," I offered with my voice.

The fruit from the fig tree dropped next to us and Cecilia dispatched her body from both me and blankets to collect us a bunch in her shirt, illuminated by the moonlight. We ate the bursting figs with our toes entwined again or we sat upright with our legs in cross-legged positions. A layer of blankets above us was our cavernous dwelling as we burst the dark flesh to get to the pulpy pink center of seeds. I fell asleep with my hand under her chin, eyes keen to continue to observe her beauty, but no longer capable.

Chapter Five

In the morning Edna did not wake me up. My father woke me up. "Your mom is in the former Union."

"Russia?" I asked.

He sighed and put his hand on his temples, "No, the former Union."

Cecilia woke up, aroused by his intrusion. She asked me to let her rest her head in my lap. I let her do that and followed the black tidal waves of her hair with my hands. She put herself even closer to me, wrapping up like a fetus while I finished the figs. I thought to offer one to my dad.

Instead, I told him, "I already have it figured out, Dad. This man deserves our love. With some of the magic I've seen her mom do," I started to turn towards Cecilia but his voice was arresting and I stopped.

He guffawed, "Do you hear what you sound like right now?"

I woke myself up to speak, "Are you going to seek out a vendetta or are you going to go against this sea of sorrows, and by opposing, end them?" I smiled gingerly, wondering if he had caught the near-quote.

His face was scornful, "You read too much at school. You've read more than your mother and I have read combined," he extended a maw to Cecilia and shook it, smiling genuinely but quickly.

"Well you had me there for a reason, right?" I asked resentfully.

"What do I do, then?" He asked, raising his arms, "Watch you work wonders?"

"Well," I didn't think he knew how close to the truth he was, "that might be it. You're a lot of energy to move, Dad. To ask everyone that is already helping to get your help, at this last and final moment, is a lot."

"A lot of energy to move, huh? What did they teach you at all of those schools?" he looked away from me as he spoke.

The pragmatist in me told me to hold my tongue and simply ask him, "Could you just be backup today outside of the cafe? Stake it out," he gave me a disgruntled look, "or whatever you call it." He nodded, smiling sadly before letting me bring him into the kitchen.

I then woke up Cecilia and my dad with coffee. He was seemingly happy to see Cecilia, bringing her in to hug her, but spoke of worry and concern.

"What would you do, Dad?" I asked him.

"Kill him," my dad snarled and I thought of the justice in that.

"You just want to teach him a lesson," I stated.

"No, a lesson would mean he goes on to live another day. Do not let him stay on this earth, Ryan. He doesn't deserve that."

"Why are you here?" I asked him, unwisely thinking of his brain tumor and the pain.

"Because your mom," he began, then stopped. "Because neither of us can deal with this, Ryan, and I wanted to make sure it wasn't too much of a burden on you to do it for us, which you don't have to, you know."

I looked up to see the eyes and nose I had inherited on a face that was not mine. "Alright, Dad. I can. I have a great group of people that can, too."

He raised an eyebrow in speculation, "Some are just as naive of novices as me, and some know what they're doing," I looked at Cecilia, who remained indifferent on the cushions.

He nodded solemnly, "You think they'll be able to kill him?"

I laughed and shook my head, "I sincerely hope not."

He finishing his coffee and let his eyes roam the kitchen languidly, "I'll get Jake and Ellsie back when you're finished," he said the last word with a clipped tone and I wondered how many people he had finished.

"Remember your words of acknowledgement when I hesitated and you asked for my help, that the responsibility of children is to do better than their parents had."

"You make me nervy," he said with an agitated tone.

Cecilia, watching him go, asked, "Is he a spy or something?"

I laughed it off and spent the morning tracing her hips with my finger while she traced her fingers around the rim of her coffee cup.

Ellsie came down the stairs first, toting a medicine bag on her waist with blue and red beads dangling from it and a long eagle feather sprouting from the center. She had with it a thumb piano and a shaker made from gourds. Edna was behind her with a drum and a smile.

They made a parade of their entrance into the kitchen. Edna began muttering ingredients to herself as she set them on the counter and put a kettle on the stove. Ellsie chewed her lip and looked over Edna's shoulder. Cecilia watched her speculatively and I wondered what it would feel like to be jealous or concerned about a person entering your mom's life.

"I heard the monkeys getting excited on the lawn last night," Edna said to us once her cup of medicinal tea was made. I looked to Cecilia to keep from smiling and she squeezed her shoulders together.

"So?"

Edna nodded and cooled her tea with her breath, "So."

Cecilia bopped her shoulders again before going to the backyard. I was getting up to follow her when she came back in, bringing in the yellow trumpet flower with her.

Edna raised her eyebrows and I watched the two exchange glances, then whispers. Ellsie made Edna laugh when she began playing a chime attached to the underside of her arm and dancing around us with arms spread and legs pumping wildly in what could be called a dance. We all seemed to be waiting for Jake and Simon because we put on coats and hats as soon as they came bubbling down the stairs, with the two dogs playing behind them as they tumbled towards us. Clearly they were enjoying rekindling the flame.

We flocked out, past graffiti, project blocks, and corner stores towards the cafe. The wind did not lift the fog but carried us through it. Children bundled in colorful jackets with bulky backpacks shuffled towards school together. We went past the school where geese still lay drowsing in the dewy marsh landscape of the playground and their own poop. We passed corner patches of greens in the ghetto—plots devoted to farming in the neighborhood. When we finally stood outside the cafe door, Simon unlocked it and swept us in. He turned on lights with magnetizing clicks and warmed up machines with whirs. Out of habit he stocked the milk and made us all eggs in bread, a popular breakfast item, on the electric skillet. When the espresso machine was hot we drank that. We were drinking a second round when there came a knocking at the door.

"Sol, how are you?" asked Simon, opening the door. Sol was wearing a sleeveless Hawaiian shirt and rain pants today, holding her fists at her sides and wearing a grimace, as per usual.

She began with a grunt and continued to say, "I'm good but I got a feeling to check in." She looked up and downy he cafe, taking us all in.

Simon tried to explain, so I waited for him to finish before I said, "Today somebody that has hurt will be shown the way and given opportunities to rebuke his own actions." Sol nodded. She had an easy way of hurry about her.

"I can and—given the way I was guided here—should help. I have been a practicing priestess. Many ceremonies in my day."

I heard Edna go, "Ooh?"

"Yeah," I said, "I don't have a plan so all the help we can get is beneficial."

She smiled, "I'm going to set up in the back," and she bustled out the backdoor. Flowing around the room, Edna was salting the ground and letting blue, violet puffs of smoke rise from tiny objects that she held in her hand.

Cups of the kava tincture in honey were passed around and the taste of it numbed my mouth. Everybody began ruminating deeply in their own ways. Jake and Simon talked and watched one another and made some elaborate plans. Elsie sat heavy-lidded and made no motion of the eyes or body. Cecilia and Edna moved as a unit.

Cecilia touched my back, "Eat this," she told me as she handed me a yellow trumpet flower.

I tilted my head, "Why? What will this do?"

"You need to," she said. I took a bite of its thin, leathery petal.

She smiled, "Now drink this."

"What is it, though?"

"Evening trumpet flower is one name for it."

"Am I going to die?"

"You very well could," she said with seriousness laced in her eyes.

"We all will."

She had handed me tea and I drank it all in three gulps, happy to rid my mouth of the taste of the Brugmansia flower.

With ease and grace, Edna had transformed the landscape of the cafe. Red and gold silks hung from the ceiling, candles flickered with altars of spiritual leaders and an assortment of deities above them. Crystals hummed energy out as I took it in. The space breathed in a wind and breathed it out. Fabrics sparkled as the rising sun pierced the fog, leaked into the cafe and onto the veils of cloth. Then the windows steamed and a fog descended on the room. A few patrons had tried to knock at the door and we had ushered them away. A quiet settled into the room. Lights flickered low as someone tried the door, realized it was locked, then, somehow, opened it anyway.

A six-foot tall man walked in the door, wearing a flowing coat, scarf, and tight paisley pants. He pocketed a snap pick, torsion wrench, and his left hand in his coat pocket. It was Leonard. The man that had had my cousins killed. The picture my dad had shown me didn't show the black canine he had in his teeth or the way a scar above his eye made the lid droop dramatically. It was him, though, I could tell that easily.

His voice gained the depth of a sinking ship as he spoke, "My machine is supposed to be here."

"No, you're supposed to be here," I said.

He looked around the space, alarmed. When his eyes passed over the warm colors of clothe. He breathed in once, looking perturbed. I wondered if he expected to smell the same thing I had smelled when I went into my cousins' house. He settled in his shoes a little as he breathed deeper and I, too, could smell the calming scents he smelled. When he closed his eyes to blink, Edna moved quickly towards him, by the third time, she was behind him, hands under his arms. For a moment, he looked at us, shocked, like he was asking us to act for him and take her out. I smiled back at him as Edna looked like she was carrying him around during a water massage. He grew limp in her arms and she sang to him deeply.

"What is this?" He asked, bemusedly.

"Sit down, there is a beautiful memory in your mind and I want you to think about it." He smiled as I breathed in to continue talking, but then bit my tongue as his smile deepened.

"Think of that favorite memory," I said, "imagine your whole being swelling with it as you breathe in and when you breathe out, I want you to think of all of the things you feel you should not have done." Despite the assumption that I had that he would grow frustrated at himself as he did so, the smile on his face grew wider and wider. "That's it," I said, "Breathe out anything you do not need to hold onto. Any bad memories that are sitting in your mind, not helping anyone. Then breathe in the memory you enjoy the most," I told him.

He smiled again, as if in a trance about good barbecue. I smiled and looked at Cecilia, who smiled good-naturedly.

Edna and I held him at the elbows and Sol touched his forehead as we led him to a pair of velvet cushions to sit on.

"This is helping you," I said as Edna moved languidly into his peripherals to touch his forehead.

She rested her index finger there only a moment before speaking, "This a paradise. Every footstep we take should be to make a positive impact on everything around us. The whole of nature is a metaphor for the human mind and I believe it. Ralph Waldo Emerson said that and it is true, which worries me. I see feet trampling along in paradise, making it a metaphor about the psychosis of the human mind. The problems do not exist until you act them out."

He sighed deeply and Edna smiled, looking around at us until her eyes settled on Sol, who nodded curtly. We watched him like parents watching a sleeping baby as he breathed in and out deeply for a few minutes. Ellsie used her instruments and Sol chanted and Edna rubbed the Wakken Takken feather I had picked up across his forehead and chest, down his legs, then back up to place it on his neck and chest. He smiled in his relaxation.

Edna and Sol exchanged looks after a few moments of rhythm and chanting and showy dancing around Leonard, then Sol held his hands as she spoke to him, "I am going to walk backwards and I want you to walk with me."

We followed the pair as they walked outside. Sol began busying herself over a large rectangular swath of black, red, lively coals. Edna moved with Leonard and Sol until they were sitting next to the coals that were burning against the pale dirt. Edna sat down, contemplating the scene in her mind. Sol's feet were bare and she removed Leonard's shoes easily.

Then I stepped in, "Imagine yourself walking along clouds, there are beautiful colors and shapes. Your favorite smell fills your nose." I suddenly saw hawks, screeched and shapes started to wiggle out of the steam from the coals. Sol stepped in where Edna had stood with Leonard. She was diminutive compared to him, but she held herself tall while his shoulders slumped.

She grabbed his hands rougher than Edna had, but was already walking along the coals. His feet eased with her. Dark, vivid worms came from the coals and wiggled over and around their feet, which were now placidly walking along them.

I continued, "Imagine yourself now higher up, walking among clouds. You are on the god-plane, where you can always go, to filter your thoughts, find patience, among other needs of your journey in peace and Nirvana, which you do not need to attain," I felt his energy release. The hawks landed on the coals and began carrying them away.

"Your journey in Nirvana has already been secured."
They came off of the coals and sat in prayer next to
Edna.

"To feel the karmic establishment of reincarnation
open yourself to the awareness of this life as a stepping
stone to Buddhahood. You may not attain it this lifetime,
but be virtuous and righteous to push to greater heights
the proximity to Buddhahood in the next lifetime
growing." Leonard Kiljun seemed to be gone. The man
that walked into the cafe was extinguished in the fire and
had become, before us, a wholly different being—just a
human.

Edna had been laying down next to him and now
moved towards him, pushing him down to a laying
position. She put both hands on his chest and began
combing at it like there were cobwebs and put her face
on his chest, sucking at it, spitting on the ground. I
watched her do this, as the hawks kept taking the coals,
Cecilia and Ellsie sang, and Jeff chanted.

The smoke from the dying embers encircled us. I
laid down as well and, upon relaxing my mind, found
myself going into a prehistoric cave. Drawings of animals
adorned the walls. I walked through the cave for a long
time, dipping and falling through cracks until I got to a
shelf of the crust, where magma flowed. I looked around
it to see spiders crawling out of the cracks in the wall.
Hawks swooped in and consumed them. I looked around
more to see snakes atop the magma, which a dozen of
the white ferrets attacked. I smiled appreciatively as all
but one hawk and my ferret dispersed. Both approached
me. The ferret crawled up me to sit in my white hoodie's
pocket and the hawk landed on my shoulder. "Go up,"
they both said. I threw myself above the lives of past,

where I had encountered so many others—artists, shamans, monks—to reach a new level of awareness. Their entwinement had made a spiritual trampoline for me from which to bounce to this next level of divinity. Happily walking through the clouds of this new awareness, I saw Jake and Simon wave me over as they grilled hot dogs in a ray of sunlight. My cousins were there with Jeff and Leonard, playing, shouting, giggling, and calling to me as I approached. Cecilia and Ellsie were there too.

"All you need to do is know you can go up further, be more aware" Cecilia said.

Elsie nodded, "Space and time are not scientific because we perceive them. Create as a form of your experience!" I thought about how I had once been told that thinking about quantum mechanics changes the way quantum mechanics function. Is that what she meant? If that was true, the object of my experience created a subjective change in the object itself. What I made of my experience changed me experience. Was I willing to continue in a place where that law was heightened?

We all joined together and walked up a cloud bank, which formed into canopy from which vines and hanging white lines of cloud-matter were formed. Edna sat at a wispy table underneath the hanging garden of clouds.

"This isn't a Hanging Garden of Babylon," she said while getting up and offering us chairs, "it is far from Babylon," she said, letting her words trail behind her as she moved, "This is Olympus." She leaned in close to whisper to me while the girls sat down, awestruck, "Not the top layer of all grand schema." She pulled back from her whisper and motioned for me to sit down.

I thought of what she had said and turned to Ellsie, "I have to suspend my knowledge in order to make room for faith." She nodded reverently, closed her eyes, and the light played across her face.

Edna was about to speak, heard a laughter from down another series of cloud-steps and frowned, "The Epicureans were right: the gods are much too concerned with their own pleasures to get into human affairs."

I stood back and up and smiled to them, "It's just nice to be here," I said.

Cecilia said, "It would be nice to have some food here." As she said it a bowl of fruit appeared on the table. Ellsie watched and soon a glass of water appeared next to her hand. She drank some and Cecilia took some seeds from a pomegranate before setting it back down.

"Six?" I asked Cecilia.

She smiled, "For winter."

I pulled the pomegranate towards me and took six jewel-like seeds from it, popping each one into my mouth and letting my molars crush the juicy encasings, then said, "For summer."

Edna looked down the stairs, then down a hallway, in a door, and over a bridge. She looked at me and I could hear her think, "Nobody is here."

I heard a hawk whistle and my ferret came out from a hole, carrying a note in his mouth. Gold glittering letters read; "Leonard is forgiven but no longer allowed on Earth. Four will rise in his place. You are to not meddle in their affairs like this one was meddled with."

"No good deed goes unpunished; the gods even rebuke you for being divine," Edna mused.

"What does it mean?" Cecilia asked.

"To whomever follows the gods, to he they particularly listen." Elsie said, "Homer said that."

I reflected on what I had done for the gods, and what they wanted me to do now—nothing but sit on my hands.

"Okay, so what does that mean, then?" Cecilia asked, "I can't keep doing this." As she said it, she vanished.

"Back to the Lowlands for her," Edna said as she walked up to a cloud column and passed her hand along it, watching the cloud disperse and resettle. Elsie sat in a meditative lotus position and Edna and I knew to do the same. We all meditated and when we opened our eyes, we were walking with gods of blue and elephants turned to men.

Edna told us, "Maybe at this time some of us that are trying to make good prevail need to cultivate good while there is an ebb of it."

We all sighed in unison.

"Want to see the Temple of Artemis? Those gods are a little more willing to—" as she said it, footsteps could be heard. Before our eyes was the runner, a golden beacon of creation. His eyes were heads above a normal man and they sparkled with intensity and knowledge. Height seemed flexible to him—he seemed to shrink when he approached Ellsie. At once eight feet, he became closer to six feet as he drew closer to her, met her eyes, and gestured to pick her up. He had been holding a square Eolian harp, but he placed it on the cloud table. She lifted an arm and he took her up to a second stairway and into the clouds.

Edna looked at me, "You know what is happening?"

"Not at all," I said.

"You'll find out."

When I heard Ellsie's shrill screams echo from the clouds, I slammed a hand through the clouds and felt myself tumbling away. I willed myself to stop falling away from Olympus. I chose to find Ellsie, get as close to her as I could. An image of a huge domed room with a white four poster bed in it came to mind. Ellsie was laying underneath me, clothes off. Blood smeared up her navel and my hands were on her wrists.

She looked at me, blinking, "What happened to him?" she asked.

"Who?"

"Zeus. He was—" she stopped, blushed. I thought of my position on her and got off diligently. She sat up and her clothes traveled from the sheets on their own and slipped onto her body. She didn't have to lift a thumb, but her hands began shaking now as they gripped the pieces of clothe.

"Thank you for wanting to save me," she said.

"From Zeus?"

She smiled, "There is something about getting what you want here. I got something, perhaps I wanted it." She looked at the door, as if watching her god go.

I touched her shoulder, "Are you going to be the same?"

She shook her head, "Nor do I want to be after that. How naive my life has been!" she nearly shouted. She smiled imperiously at me as I led her out the door to see that we were no longer in the clouds but among brambles and thorns. Laughter rose and a chariot parted the thorns and came upon us. I looked daunted but Ellsie smiled.

"You don't seem to be afraid," I stated as I felt myself slipping out of this plane and into another.

"Seneca the Elder said: 'All cruelty springs from weakness.' The Gods have no weakness and therefore are not cruel. Simple logic and understanding will—"

I didn't hear her speak anything else as I changed over planes. I was in a heavily wooded, near-tropical forest. Huge trees twisted their roots down from branches to create news trees close to them. The leathery, green, elliptical leaves of the Banyan tree surrounded me. One mother Banyan tree sat in the middle and, under it, sat monks. They smiled with their Qi flows and I was instantly absorbed in them. I walked to them meditatively. I saw they were children. I realized that I was one, too. I sat down and closed my eyes. I could not see a face, but I recognized that I was sitting with a collection of Buddha. I fell in love with what I saw there, on the black of my eyelids, and knew and trusted that I would stay there for many moments past this one.

Jeff had come from within me, I knew, and would always be with me. I knew before he touched me that he was there with me, always. A hand lay on my shoulder and my senses tingled. Jeff and I smiled in unison and were alone, suddenly. The monks and jungle were gone and I looked at an open-air panorama of the universe around us. We floated in space that we had made.

I said, "Things will be different; we will have no control over what happens now."

"Yes, you must take your place in the order of nature by way of correct balance," he said as he floated to lay on his belly.

"That means-"

"That you must accept the destruction or it will consume you."

"We need to watch the destruction or there will be no balance." The sun of the galaxy we were in caught my eye—it was pulling a cluster of the planets close.

"We have created and must now let destruction purge extraneous."

"You can be a leader to others," Jeff replied.

"No," I said, watching the sun and planets' trajectories form in my mind.

"Yes," he replied, advocating against my resistance.

"Even with good intentions, misfortune will fall on a plan that is not orderly," I said, "I want action with understanding to pierce through this."

"You do not think you have enough understanding to do so?"

"I am weak, you must know that."

Jeff nodded as we floated closer to a small planet and said, "Strength can displace weakness if, like thunder and lighting, are patterned together to adjust for a greater case." We moved through the layers of planetary gravity pull. It resisted my body's own movement, like the ocean on a choppy day.

"Then I will observe weakness and draw strength," I said.

"There is water in the earth like an army." He said, "A great leader does the same as the earth to take people in and care for the masses."

"You sound like the I Ching," I said.

"I should," he said, looking at me pointedly. I laughed as we approached the planet closer. We stepped on sand to walk a length of beach on the small planet. Its sky was white and a speckling of blue dots marred a bright portion of it.

Edna was there with a white-haired luminary standing beside her. She saw me looking at the sky and nodded, "This atmosphere's condition makes the sky white, like a canvas, and the planets in this galaxy are delineating the dying sun, like a painter's splash of indigo on negative space. What a beautiful place. Boys, this is Austin Godwin," she said, putting her hands on his shoulder and elbow. "Would you care to go back now? Cecilia is very lost."

I imagined her and I standing there, happily, in the light together. She appeared on the beach and we looked toward the jungle together. I summoned my cousins and Leonard to come and they came, looking at the jungle, too, and leaping forth to play in it and explore its boundaries. The youngest, Lena, bent down to pick up the white sand and let it filter through her young hands. They were all such beautiful children and, seeing them here in heaven made hot tears trickle into my mouth. I felt it on my lips and tasted it with my tongue. I couldn't help but smile as I watched a couple of guavas hit one of my cousins on the head as they walked beneath the short trees. A few of them began collecting the pink fruit.

The oldest of them, Marvin, came forward, "Here, have this," he handed me the guava,"Thank you, Ryan."

I put my hand on his neck, feeling the soft black skin that he still had after death, choking back tears, to say, "Any time. I'll see you all when I can but until then," I looked him in his hazel eyes, "I love you. You guys keep loving while you're hanging around in every nook and cranny of the cosmos. Make something cool and I will come see what it is. Make everything you want." He nodded and ran towards the jungle. I wanted to leap after him, but I felt Jeff's hands on me, so I held back.

I beckoned Leonard over and he began thanking me. "I have this opportunity to be able to rise above who I was, what I was doing, what I was thinking." He said, speculatively, "But nothing could have changed me. You can't change other people." I looked at the stocky European man, wondering what my family had done to deserve his wrath to begin with.

I fought with words, "I knew that. That's a matter of fact. Would you change yourself, though?"

He looked around contentedly, "I don't really have the opportunity now, do I?"

My eyebrows knit together, "Are you saying this because you know you won't be going back to Earth?"

He looked baffled, "You killed me," he said.

Leonard still had many cycles of soul to revolve through, but here, today, on this beach, he was content and happy. Jeff's fingers pressed into my collarbone. I was not looking, but weeping softly, my eyes becoming too convoluted with tears to see anymore. Jeff turned me away from Leonard to watch my cousins play, their shining black faces breathing excitedly as they played in the sand and swung from the trees.

My cousins screamed excitedly as they ran out of the jungle with a procession of slowly walking monks behind them. I couldn't quite tell if they were chasing my cousins in fun or just trotting around the forest, but I surmised that that was an ambiguity I didn't need to look into. I stopped asking questions and remained attached to tanning my eternal soul in the soft light of this planet. Eventually, it was time to leave.

Chapter Six

We began to awake back in West Oakland. Edna and I were close to Leonard's body. She awoke quickly and upon looking over, she began battling with a writhing mass of snakes coming from his body. To me, it seemed they were pulling him back under the ground. Their bodies slipped easily from our hands as we tried to pick up masses of them, mostly corn snakes and garden snakes that couldn't hurt us, but as we pulled them from the ground or his body, they dissipated in our hands. I wanted to squeeze them until they burst apart, but saw Edna shaking her head.

"Spirit Guides," Edna whispered to me over his body and the wriggling linear colors that were the snake guides started pulsing as my vision narrowed.

"They shouldn't be there," I said, my fingertips itching to start combing them off of his body.

She placed a hand on mine, "Do not try."

We watched the writhing snakes consume his flesh and I thought to put my hand to his jaw and check for a pulse before seeing them consume the area, then his face. They seemed to pull him under the ground with them, wiggling down into the coals before a few popped out of one area, surveyed the coals, then slid back down.

Edna sighed and I shook my head. I began digging out the coals, my fingernails scraped against the carbon and my fingertips started to hurt, but even a foot under the top layer of coals, there were still more. My knees dug into the ground as I tried to get leverage enough to dig deeper. The black of the coal began to move up my arm and I felt my head shake as I started to cry, looking down at my darkened hands and forearms. I lurched my shoulders out to continue digging again when I heard Edna's arresting voice. I sat there, shaking and listened.

"Let his body disperse back in the earth." She said sternly.

"Is that what happened?"

Edna said, "I wasn't on this plane, just like you." I sat over the pile, questioning what my intentions had been and if I had reached them. I heard a hawk whistle and looked around to see it, but the brilliant blue sky was clear. As I looked around, I saw everyone groggily waking up, except Sol, who was the epitome of chipper. I thought of the heartwood—the hard, tough, inner wood in a tree trunk. That had to be what Sol was made of to make a coal pit so deep and powerful. She took care of each of us, seeing what we each needed, and encouraging us to lay back down instead of walking about. Though Edna brushed her off, she stayed in the same place next to the pit across from me and I could hear her stifle her tears as I let my mind try to discern what I had done.

Chapter Seven

It was now late afternoon and my dad slipped into the cafe just as I walked across the boundary from the outside lot to the inside to get myself coffee.

"I had a bit of a head trip," I said as I washed my hands, regretting the words I used. He remained silent while I watched the black coal splatter the stainless steel sink and swirl down the drain. The brackish water dripped from my hands and I watched where it landed before being consumed by clean water and taken away. Only until the water that dripped from my hands was clean did I stop washing them.

"When lines are crossed during alert consciousness," he said, "Your subjective experiences play a bigger role in your functioning." He grabbed a bar stool and moved it under himself to sit down on.

I asked, "Like deviations in what you expect?" while pushing and pulling the different espresso levers.

"No, more like what you expect creates your reality."

"What is this about?"

He said, "The individual must see as an observer if he wants to be an observer."

"You're saying what?" I rubbed my hands against my thighs, which felt like they had recently run a marathon. My fingers traveled to my lower spine nodules, which felt empty and hurt to the touch. I shook my head, astounded by the pain throughout my body.

"Expectations are a little more objective with some Ludwig logic under your belt." He sighed in my silence and said, "Stay sane."

"What happened back there?" he asked and I pointed to the espresso machine, "Of course, of course, waiting is fine," he said as I poured a few shots in a cup of warm water.

"Anything I can do for you?"

"Pray."

"I'll do that when I get world peace. Not today," he said.

"Fine."

He looked up at me, curious again, "What did happen back there?" He nodded toward the back lot where everyone still sat around, groggy and hurt.

"We put him in the gods' hands." I said bitterly. I would rather see Leonard walking back to his gang to reform them before chaos ensued instead of gone. He was off of this earth. But the gods had intervened, whether or not I could explain it or accept it. I thanked mother earth and the four directions again—I hadn't seen them there, but knew they had helped.

My dad scoffed, as I expected him to and I said, "It wasn't easy getting him off the earth like you wanted." I felt like I was placing blame on his desires as I said it.

"Dead?" He asked.

"One murdering weapons distributor is gone," I said curtly.

"Good," he looked up at me with me with a smile. I turned my face, sternly eyeing him and he dropped his head.

He drummed his fingers against the bar and said, "Cut off a dragon's head and watch it grow four more."

I looked at him, grimly wide-eyed, "I think they said that would happen."

"Well, you're safe and so I have something close to good news for your aunt and mom, who I'm going to go to after I get Jake and Ellsie. What should I tell your aunt? She's heartbroken, now. Of course. But I'm glad he's dead."

"Who are you to decide?" I asked him, looking at his staunch appearance.

"I'm the one who put you on this earth and has taken hundreds off of it," he growled over to me.

"And who had you do that?" I asked.

"Our government," he said.

I laughed, "Oh yeah? Why couldn't they help you when your family was endangered?"

He set his jaw, "They don't even know, because the government has bigger problems."

I laughed, harder this time, "Big bad government can't take care of an itty-bitty criminal."

He looked stricken, "They have done everything they can to-"

I cut him off by saying, "They put an emphasis on commercial success over individual's life and liberty. Our capitalistic government is what is asking criminals to come up with insane weapons and," he began to grow red and agitated, "I know they don't ask every small-time crook if these products of death were tested on children or adults or anything."

He erupted by saying, "You don't have faith in a system I have worked for for years!"

I had been ready with words, "How can I when you abandoned me for a system and left me in another abusive one for years?"

He looked awash with emotion and said, "We wanted the best."

"Yes, for you. Never for me. The best for a child is a family and a home. Where was that? I have one, now, without you."

"Who are you to say that to me?"

"I'm the one that just found a murderer," I yelled, "I had the means to get him here, you couldn't even come ask questions, take care of him the professional way, something?"

"You're not good enough to do this alone, ever again."

"I don't want to! Never again!"

He said, "You are not my son," before turning to leave the cafe.

"At least you know where to find me when you change your mind," I yelled at his back.

My eye caught a glittering golden flash next to him as he opened the door and left. Only after it was gone did it look like a tear in the scenery zipping back up.

I sat in my own silence, growing accustomed to sounds none of my late relatives had heard: the roar of the BART tracks just above the cafe; the clicking of the espresso machine heating itself up after minutes of disuse; curse words and slang of my generation yelled on the street, all drifting into the cafe. I glanced out the window and barely saw that everyone basically had remained unmoved. Edna caught my eye and began standing up, leaning over to the coals, then placing a hand on them. I was interested, but still resolute after such a heated argument with my dad and turned away.

Edna and, to my surprise, her pale partner from the beach on the planet, strode in from the back garden lot we had inhabited.

They giggled and she cupped my hand in hers as I sat at the bar. I looked down at the soft, aged brown of her skin against the hard, shiny black of my hand. My eyes followed the lines of my wrist and forearm before I hung my head and looked in my lap. Her hand moved up to cup my chin and she leaned towards me to kiss my cheek lightly. I smelled her scent and heard her breathe. Thinking of what she and Cecilia had done for me, I looked up to gaze into her speckled robin's egg eyes. I forced a smile and she sighed, then moved to make room for me to see her companion.

"Austin, this is Ryan." She re-introduced us, then said to me, "You have never done this sort of thing?" We nodded in unison. "I saw that. You are now a rogue and a charlatan and you are a shaman of high degree—all at the same time!" She clapped her hands together excitedly. "Somehow you learned all of the perfect things, the knowledge fell into your brain about what to do. You have such a knack for it, to think the mother and creator decided to have justice be your cause. You could have been a healer, an adventurer, a conqueror of new thought! Oh, well."

It did not feel like enough to call a skill-set. I wondered if anything was enough with a parent's love and knew the answer without thinking back on my years of abandonment.

She became ecstatic and Austin put a hand on her hip, "Slow down," he gazed at me, then her, and said, "What ought to happen doesn't always happen, especially when benevolent forces are at work." He smiled and the lights of the room brightened.

"Why hasn't this ever happened to me before?" I asked, sort of clenching and unclenching my hands in front of me.

Austin put a hand on them, "Like I said, not everything that can happen or ought to happen, does."

"So because it needed to happen, it did?" I asked.

Edna smiled and laughed and Austin said, "She had more to do with it happening that way than you did."

"Oh," I said, deflated. "This wasn't me finding out I have had magic in me all along," I began, but they both frowned, "Okay, so we all have magic in us, but this wasn't me finding out that I am an extra-special magic master, was it?"

Edna frowned even more, "I am only a master because I have put hundreds of hours of practice into it."

Austin put a hand on my shoulder, "You're not a master of anything yet, especially something you just tried."

Edna changed the conversation, "You know I got to know Leonard quite well up there." She smiled inwardly.

I shrugged, "I didn't see you two together."

She blew out a breath of air, "Well, you weren't there, where you?"

"I'm going to check on Cecilia and Ellsie. Thank you, for everything." She nodded and I left through to the back. Outside, the back of the cafe had a reconstructed tug boat in it, its green outer walls sun-bleached pale and its inner walls, rusted. It sat atop stacks of weeds and long grasses. Next to it lay an abandoned chicken coop and a poorly planted plot of dying autumn harvest plants.

Sol exclaimed as she saw me, "Hello! Nice work."

"Let's not talk about crimes a mere man has punished," I said off-handedly.

"Okay."

I pointed to the boat, which Cecilia and Ellsie now sat on, "What's that?"

"An artist's statement piece next to a cross-section of back lots and tumbleweeds in Oakland's most gentrified, impoverished area." Her statement about the piece was derailing in contrast the joyful sight of the tug boat. I looked around at the lot.

"Who owns this, Sol?"

"A good friend of mine owns this entire block of houses and the lot."

"I want to talk to him," I said.

She nodded towards the tug boat, "I'll set something up."

I let myself disengage and walk towards the girls, which had slowed their talk to watch me cross the grass to them.

The boat was a light aquamarine that had been dug partly into the ground so that there was a dirt floor under a large area in the hull and the deck of it. Inside the bottom portion of it golden rods of sun held sparkling veils of yellow light that fell from them. They illuminated sections of the boat's innards. The inside of the hull was rusted red and painted over in part with a rainbow palette of graffiti and white wheat-pasted paper designs. The white paper eccentrically enveloped a corner and hung limply at the edges.

"What, is this a troller?" I asked about the boat to Cecilia and Ellsie above me.

Red-rusted bars had been welded onto the aquamarine metal below where they sat. They dangled their feet over the side of it. I stood outside of it, on the raised platform.

It would have done a quite splendid job of lifting fish if it were a troller.

Their ankles and hair were all that I saw of the girls as I looked up. Ellsie bounced her feet and Cecilia's were crossed. I averted my eyes to look at the rusted metal of the boat's guts. I saw the inner parts differently; it had been wounded by the tangential graffiti and wheat pasted patterns of adult-onset ADHD fits. The artist's process here was more beautiful than the product.

I looked up and watched their dangling feet. They both leaned over together to at first show me only their chins.

Ellsie spoke as she looked at me more, "Crimes not punishable by mere man?"

"You heard that," I began to say, but stopped due to lack of self-faith.

Ellsie flipped herself backwards on the troller and probably was there like a martyr with her arms flopped to either side. Two perpendicular lines joined at one axis to a bisecting line. I couldn't see her, though, so I only imagined her laying there like a martyr.

I stopped. Breathed in a breath of my favorite memory, its imagery and sounds and smells, then breathed out my least favorite memory. I continued restraining myself with forced meditation. Then, after really controlling my thoughts I thought about just how much our generation had been taught.

What I had been taught and what everybody around me knew. There was no reason to not abolish the old systems that did not work. I wanted to forget the concept of hiring a genius like Albert Einstein to develop the A then not take his philosophical and political understanding, as well. The consequences, both good and bad, should have had been affected by his genius, as well. But they were not taken into account, the systems had decided to use it on Japan without his philosophical or political expertise considered.

That concept was one I didn't want to be a part of. The system that left him depressed and overly self critical for months to come was not one that I saw working for anyone very well or very long. I wanted to live within a system that can then ask for sociological and philosophical input from him.

Cecilia looked at me, her black mane of curls on her head swayed in turmoil. I looked into the boat and saw panels of light streaming in. The grime of the dirt on the floor of it was illuminated in the sunset. It almost sparkled golden as the sun shifted against it. Two large entrances had been cut from the steel and the setting sun was settling in to the patchy grass and dirt mess. Light glinted off of cobwebs and soda or beer cans. In a corner, I saw a bottle filled with vinegar and two rattle-snakes. The paper designs hung limply in spots of the design.

Again, though, I appreciated the illumination provided. Ayn Rand had written about this. Dominque, the female lead, writes for a journal about a certain Howard Roark's artistry in his field. She admits he illuminates a patch of humanity through art that is comparable to a pig sty, but mysteriously includes no hint of admiration for him. Instead, she criticizes the pig

sty for being there. I understood this being the point
where the public misunderstands her criticism, which is
really directed at them. They begin to revolt against
Howard, a man who is only in it for the mastery over his
craft. Her journal article was a catalyst for many clients
abandoning Roark. They go to the professionals that
stick to preclassical. He had studied. He had read and
researched. He was influenced in order to create. She
loved him.

This public outcry against him necessitated
Dominique to protect him from the public's scorn,
although it was born from her. Howard was like a light,
she said, illuminating what shouldn't be there. What
shouldn't be there, the pig sty that was humanity,
detested the light through their own confusion.

Rand wrote an industrial romance in a very modern
world. I wanted that, I thought, as I looked at Cecilia. I
didn't want the pig-sty of humanity and I had to thank
the illumination for being able to see it.

I looked up to see the light glimmering off of
Cecilia's rotund locks of hairs. I saw the sun illuminate
her, showing only brilliance and beauty.

"What are you thinking?" I asked Cecilia.

She groaned audibly, "I hate when people ask me
that."

A fast wind picked up to push me around as I spoke,
"I want to know your whims. I can't just think of what I
want when I'm one of an entire forest, meaning you and
everyone else."

She scoffed.

My frustration made me ask, "Why am I validating
such an innocent thing?" I shook my head soothingly as
my words visibly scalded her, "An innocent question

doesn't need that amount of validation. I don't want you to make me feel wrong for an innocent thing."

Ellsie leaned forward and to me, said, "If the tree wanted anything, such as the most sunlight, to never get tangled with another tree, or for an over-abundance of water, it could not function in the whole." She flopped back down as quickly as she had gotten up.

I looked at Cecilia and said, "Being a good individual adds to being there for the whole."

She seemed to scoff as her body swayed in a turmoil, "I'm not going to tell her that," she said with a hot anger.

She seemed upset. I quickly thought about what I could have said to upset her. That feeling alone made me feel revolted in the stomach.

"The intonation of what you just said made me feel-" I began to say, before she cut me off.

"What the fuck did you just say to me?" She asked.

"I wish you could know how little I like hearing cursory words." I managed to say.

"I don't give a fuck," she said.

Ellsie was sitting up and I was able to look away from Cecilia, who had acquired a sharpness to her features and presence that was driving me mad. I made to leave when I heard her voice yell to me, which made me pause and turn back to them.

"How are you so okay after all of that? Both of us," she pointed to Ellsie, "had to fight to get back to Earth and are hurt now." She looked down at Ellsie's belly, then at the palms of her own hands, "But you, you're just as fine as could be. Not hurt at all like us."

"I'm sorry?" I tried.

"How I took on so much a burden from what we just did, I don't know but, it hurts," she was nearly growling out words again.

Ellsie chirped at her, "You are not liable for what is out of your control, even if you are able to observe it," she finished by jumping up and walking along the top of the boat before pausing abruptly and putting her hand to her forehead. She used her palm to shield her eyes as she looked out to the horizon.

Cecilia said, "Even if you performed actions that led to it?"

"Uh-huh," Ellsie said distractedly.

"Ellsie?" Cecilia said.

"Yes?" She replied quickly, optimistically.

"I live in the now, not the Dao." With a swift set of movements Cecilia had jumped down and had her hands in her pockets like she was going to walk past the green field, school, and housing projects to her home.

I gave a low grumble and Ellsie looked at me, saying chipperly, "Behave to get the greatest pleasure. See what it is like to be utilitarian."

There are contingent aspects of the world, like what could have been different.

There are fixed, necessary aspects that are not different.

Contingent.

Necessary.

"There are things we can know," Ellsie began, "and things we should try to know."

"Enough Kant, Ellsie!" I spat at her.

"But it wasn't," she tried to deny.

"It was *Critical Systems*, Ellsie," I said sternly as I watched her body change into one that was withdrawing and no longer receptive.

"You're right, but the moral law is within me while the starry heaven's above. Not even you can stop that." She had flipped on a facade with words, then faltered when she said, "I'm going to go look for my dad."

My first impulse was to recite what I had been taught, "Beliefs most vulnerable are the ones that have not been attacked before." I continued to watch her, "Because nobody has attacked them before, the individual has not built up resistance to it," I tried to catch her, net her, ensnare her, with the words but she seemed steadfast in her decision to leave.

"Though I am sure you have had ten times the number of teachers as I, " she told me, "I still wonder how you could be so ignorant."

"In my experience, I've felt desensitized to people after they call me names like that," I lifted myself up on a piece of the boat, as I spoke.

Finally standing after sitting so still, Ellsie was up, squatting, she grabbed the bars of metal at the top of the ladder of the boat. She turned her hips and legs to start a descent down. Her feet slipped off and on each bar quickly, making soft sounds of movement. She twirled and left.

I laughed as I realized I had just scared two girls away because I was scared, myself.

Chapter Eight

My energy felt low enough to not be brightened by a
thing. I wanted to curl up and sleep off my lethargy for
life. Reinstitute my raison d'être with a Renaissance
before lunch tomorrow. Knowing I had an emptiness, I
turned to where we had all been together. Earlier it had
been full, now it was only a grassy field empty of us.

I turned from it and cut across the field to the side of
the boat. I went over the chain-link fence and onto 8th
street. I took a few right turns on foot, walking past
people of all ages that hung around the sidewalks.

From them, paint usually was pushed on the walls
while shiny plastic packages fell from their hands to the
gutters. What they got was little, though, so the idea that
they were over-disposing of anything too much didn't
matter yet.

It would matter when the rest of the people of this
world could stop being so distressed over the ghetto and
start feeling some empathy for the people living in it.

Like I had said to Ellsie, there were some ways of
desensitizing people with weak arguments or strong
words. People can build up walls to beliefs if weak

arguments for them are followed up by counter-arguments. A group can do this and make a better image for themselves. You can argue in manner that appears against your own self-interest to make more of an impact on your audience. I had some nasty, manipulative tools like those at my feet, but I didn't want to pick them up.

Sometimes, not choosing the schemes that feel dirty and wrong were part of the reason that problems stewed. I tapped my fingers against my thigh as I thought on it. There were a myriad of problems that could, and historically have, been unsuccessfully solved. With simple and limited opinions like mine, the struggles of poverty were washed away with the causes of poverty, and the cycle would continue again.

I said to myself as a comfort, "'Look at the past cultures- how they rose, and fell, and you will see what the future holds,'" which was a loose quote of Marcus Aurelius'.

The people here were not characterless. They were not angry or mean. They were not hurt or helpless. They were invisible, though. Society had already decided what Oakland was. What it had to offer was decided and defined without a glance at them.

"Oh, you're from Oakland?" people would say to Tre, reviling him. I felt they blamed him and me for being there, blamed for occupying a place that America had turned its back on. Like Detroit, where few were building anything new, Oakland was becoming a place where the good that was there was being stamped out. Nobody talked of what it could be based on the good that was there, they talked about what it was that made it bad and how it would continue in the same thread.

The leaves on the streets' trees seemed to be eternally moving, quivering on the branch- tentative to see if they wold be falling or growing. When they fell, they were crisp and golden, like pages of a book that had been saturated and dried. And when they were growing, they just looked saturated.

They made my questions about what could work for every person how to add to everybody's lives here- not only some less prominent people, a heavy question on my mind.

The trees all sat in large beds of soil, tumors on the sidewalk's plain spine. In some of them were more ornamental bushes, some had patchy grass, and one had a man in a wheelchair. He sat there when the weather wasn't bad and would make conversation. The first time he talked to me, he yelled from the sidewalk about the book in my hand.

"I've seen you walking with your nose in that book for a week," he said, pointing and laying his hand back in his lap calmly, "What's it for, school?"

"Not school," I shook my head, "me."

"Well then, you must be pretty smart," he said.

"Nope," was my reply. He wouldn't take that for an answer, though.

"You doing okay, though? Know enough about the neighborhood?" He rubbed his thigh with just one hand while wincing.

"Are you asking because I'm-" I started to ask, but his face changed and I stopped immediately when I noticed.

"Enough with that," he started yelling. "It's because I haven't seen you with one single friend. You lived here what, awhile!"

"What's your name?" I asked.

"Charles," he said, while picking the bottoms of his sleeves from his wrists and pulling them to his elbows.

"Well now I know you but, I don't know much about the neighborhood, no."

"You know just as much about is as you know about yourself," he said with the lids of his eyes dragging against the pupils, lifting to almost look at me before looking away. I felt like he was intentionally shaming me. I wondered if he speculated that because I didn't know myself, I wouldn't try to get to know my surroundings, or that because I didn't already look around myself, I wouldn't want to look inward either.

"Let me tell you," he said, "whatever you're doing- it's wrong."

I had been taken aback that first day. Mostly, that night, I thought about the loneliness he had given me. I had not regretted it before, but, now that I thought about it, it was there. Where before there was an empty place that I enjoyed roaming freely in, I wanted it filled with something I did not know about.

There was no escape from some of life's pain, not even with others. Inevitably, I found one must face life alone no matter how close you get to others and take responsibility for the direction of your own life no matter how much support or guidance you get from others.

I felt ashamed for overlooking my own insignificant impact on the world around me.

Today, he asked how I was and I said, "Got knocked around a bit."

"Did it hurt?" He asked.

"Well, it didn't tickle," I said, thinking of a boxer.

He nodded and grumbled while saying, "Been there. Grip it well."

"What?" I could finally ask the questions with Charles.

"Keep your grip on life," he explained.

I said blankly, "I thought you said I didn't have one."

He laughed and held onto the wheels of his chair, "Well neither do I! I only have a grip on these and even then that doesn't get me anywhere!" He laughed in a way that made me know we were done talking, we were both heavy with self-reflection and neither liked to talk after that.

I put my head down as I walked away, heavy with preoccupying thoughts.

It is natural to attribute actual reality to new forms of perception. There could be different reasons for what we did, but I didn't want to try too hard to hold the answer that I broke it while grabbing for it. If I didn't yet have all of the answers, a few of them were at least within my grasp or in my hand.

Soon I was at my car's lot and in it, head on the steering wheel and breathing heavily.

I thought of my decimated apartment, which was ransacked and probably known to all of Leonard's conspirators. I had to move, and I could tell I wouldn't be moving out of the neighborhood as I thought about Charles in his chair, Cecilia up the street, the cafe, Simon, Edna; all of them meant too much to let them think I could live a life without them.

A knock came to my door, Sol was slightly bent at the hips, asking me to open my car door.

"Hey, honey," she said.

"Hey, flour," I replied.

She opened her mouth and her eyebrows dug into her sunglasses, "What?"

"It was a joke-" I tried to think of a way to explain, "Ingredients, like, honey, sugar, flour."

"Well," she chuckled, "I just don't think I get it. Anyway, I remember you asking about the building behind the cafe. Do you want the number for the owner?"

"Course!" I said, chipperly noting how things work out so well and so quickly.

"Well, here it is," she showed me the number on her phone and I looked for mine to type it into.

"Helping is a great way to draw anyone out of self-absorption," she continued to talk of a relatable story, but I only stared at the number I had typed.

"What makes you say that?" I asked.

"I have been watching you," she alluded as she looked around the street. "You know, coming in and out of the cafe and while you talk to others. You are, like all of us, interested in yourself. Maybe too interested in yourself. You watch others as they react to you, but not as they think of themselves. You-" she hesitated as I realized just how shallow my introspection was if she was able to do it so much better for me, "-you changed that today, you know. This morbid self-absorption is gone. I can tell."

I knew not what to do to hold the lesson in my hand, while still thanking her for giving it to me. She trotted off before I could, waving to a woman walking with her child and looking around herself, pleased with the scenery.

There was little to do but go ahead and call him.

The beeps were slow and soft before a man picked up and answered. "Hello, this is Artie."

"Hi Artie, I was just talking to Sol," I started.

"Oh?" he said, "Let her know I give her my best."

"Will do. For now, I have a question for you about the house behind the cafe, the green one."

"Oh?"

"Well, I like it. Something about it interested me and it looks disused now."

"It is," he laughed into the receiver.

"Well, is it in good enough condition to rent?" I asked.

He laughed, "Nope. Close but nope. No heating, washer, dryer, bad plumbing, you know?"

"I can add to it." I tried, "Fix it up for you."

"Don't say you'll do things you can't do."

I replied, "But I can. Repairs, additions, the like."

He laughed again, but I could hear him breathe in heavily. "You know what, kid, what's your name?"

"Ryan," I said.

"Great, you have a deal, Ryan."

I nodded, but realized I needed to say, "Sounds good."

"Good, get me on this number anytime. Talk to Sol about keys and stuff. Nobody is a tenant there currently. Talk to you when I talk to you next," and he clicked the phone off.

I sat in my car, head on the steering wheel and eyes closed. The sun moved in to hit my head, then torso, with its light, which was harsh and deterred me from moving in it anymore than I had to. I liked it more when the sun hit my skin and it got an unraveling feeling. That day, that time, that place all helped me feel like I was being rubbed by a cilice when I wanted it to be wrapped by silk.

Sweat sprouted under my arms. The edges of my vision became dark and yellow. Looking around me and focusing on the center of my vision was like trying to hold an ice block with my bare hands. My hands began working without me, and I let them. I had to trust myself while letting myself escape inside my own mind. My fingers fumbled with metal and I thought I could taste in my mouth the grey metal as the sweat on my fingertips touched them.

I put the key in the ignition of the car, ready to remove the metaphorical hair shirt of heat. I let the battery turn on, which registered the A/C, which pushed forth air, billowing at me. It felt like wet sheets hanging on a clothesline flapping in the wind. I moved my head slowly, shaking it and letting the air wrap around me.

It hurt. It stung. It felt like ice forming in me and melting and then, reclaiming the pores on my skin as their own to form icy layers again. And then, they would melt again. I thought of Cecilia, of her stark body receding away from me. I thought of Cecilia, coming now, to warm me for good, to blow fresh air on my face and push my hair away from my face. I lifted my hand to do it myself, but it fell to my lap, closing around nothing and doing nothing. Like myself, I must have thought. It was like myself to be doing nothing for myself.

Adornments had been put up. Embellishments to look at when I felt too much. The image of my hand outside of a car window, sweeping and gliding on the air as it moved around me, as the earth moved around the sun which was setting against the horizon. That image was ripped from the wall of my mind. A moment in time, when a teacher had asked me to stay after class, had praised me, had told me I should be proud, was gone. The thoughts, those thoughts, that helped me all my life forgive and forget, were pulled out of my heart. The adornments and embellishments I had spent a lifetime putting there. The objects on the wall of my heart that I always knew should be there were immediately ripped down.

A breath sputtered out of me and I listened to its struggle. What was wrong with me to stop me from doing my first function so poorly, I thought, as my entire body became warped. As the last bit of air left with that breathe, my belly started shaking and my head was in my hands, which were open and holding tightly, by the fingertips, my mind.

I let slip the cold memories of loneliness and abandonment in a boarding school that felt more like an orphanage than a home. Reassuringly, I thought that it was more of a safe-house for me now that I knew who they were. Years of thinking my parents did not want me would not be erased as easily as the defenses and walls I had structured. Years of being afraid and alone were visible again.

In me was nothing. I gasped violently as I remembered only knowing that there used to be something there. Things I had made that could bloom and erupt with passion and happiness.

My fingers gripped the plastic butt of the ignition key, turning it gradually until I could hear the sound of the transmission from the engine bay, to the inner of the car, then to me. I registered its movement, its resonance moving the car lightly. I had always liked the rocking movement of cars and busses. When the residential coordinators took us places on our days off, the slow rocking of the vans and busses would send me to sleep. Then, in the car, I felt the same comforting movement of the space around me. I checked around me, looking dazedly and running my wrists against both eyes. I pushed in the button on the e-brake, lifted it, and slowly rocked my foot into and off the brake pedal. I gassed it and moved the wheel to go into the street. It glided, like a bead on a tilted plate, falling slowly, then fast.

I gasped for air and stopped all of the thoughts. I made room in my mind only for numbers, now, counting to without thinking about the numbers I was on nor the number I would get to. The sun started to touch me more gently and I felt like I was drinking lemonade instead of eating a whole lemon. I felt better. Not whole, but not broken anymore.

I had systematically driven to my apartment and I found myself emptying it, three small armfuls in all, and driving it back to the westside of Oakland. There, I parked outside the quaint green house, with its rod-iron fence and walnut tree in the ten-foot front yard. I unlatched the gate and walked up the steps, setting my things by the front door and pulling from the pile two small, nondescript pieces of metal I had been sent long-ago. I went to the left of the house, which was flanked by a wooden fence. On the other side of that fence was the lot and, as I walked closer to the back of the house, I could see the green top of the boat ascending into view.

I tucked myself against the back door, sliding the metal tension wrench against the adjoining wood and pushing the thin cylinder into the keyhole. The lock gave up its secret and gave me access. I pocketed both items and walked in, inspecting the house, which was on the better side of disrepair. The back door led into a small alcove, with a tiny, doorless bathroom and an oversized cleaning sink. A few bottles of colorful cleaning liquid sat underneath. From there, a doorway to the right of the door led to the kitchen, with its own large, but barred, windows. I opened the refrigerator to find nothing but a clean, white interior. I went into the living room, the room closest to the front porch, then unlocked the series of locks on the front door. I opened the door to see a man huddled over my pile of goods.

"Hey," I said, not knowing what I would try to say to deter him. He was wearing a red sweater with moth holes and black grease stains with baggy, torn pants.

"Oh, hey, man. I didn't know anyone was living here now. I wouldn't have done a thing if-"

I put up a hand and smiled, "I get it. But, yeah, that is my stuff." I hesitated, then asked, "Take anything?"

He looked to his right, said, "No," then waved his hand, "well, have a good day anyway." He stepped down from the porch and hopped the small brick wall that separated our yard from the one next to it. I thought I could call after him, try to talk him into proving some kind of guilt, but I knew there was no good in that. It would be like beating a dead horse, which sounds a lot better than beating a live one, but was still something I didn't need to do.

I put my bags just inside the door and went inside, locking the door behind me. I checked the upstairs, the hot water, and electricity and went back the way I came. Instead of going back to my car parked outside the house, I jumped the back fence and landed on a tussock. I picked myself up, making sure nothing had spilled out of my pockets and into the stiff grass, then strode up to the boat, where I held the rods of the ladder welded into the metal frame in my hand and climbed up. The air was cooler and as I lifted my head to the top, it blew in my face and I smelled in it jasmine. Turning, Cecilia looked at me.

Her hands were clasped around her legs and her chin rested on her knees. He hair rose and fell in the wind, quick to be picked up and heavy enough to fall down just as quickly. I smiled hesitantly and when she did not smile back, I let the happiness I had mustered fade. I sat near her, looking the same direction she was looking.

She seemed to decide on the lines she would use and spoke, "Did anyone ever tell you that you were intelligent and nice?"

I thought on it and spoke with humiliated honesty, "No."

She shook her head while speaking, "Then what gave you the idea that you were?"

Shocked, I stared at her. My mouth was open but no words came. I watched her beauty fade in front of me. The soft lines of her face and the glow her skin reflected all seemed so distant and untouchable.

She turned to me, her eyes a well of emotion that I had no bucket to dip in to take from it, "I didn't mean that."

"You said it, Cecilia; you meant it when you said it."

"I just," she hesitated and grabbed a lock of hair to entwine it in her fingers, "I just think there are things about you I don't know what to do with."

"You don't need to do anything, Cecilia. I do. These problems of mine will occupy my head for the rest of my life. I hope I always have them, because the more I have to change in myself, the less likely I am to start to notice the problems of the people around me. I don't want to think about the problems I see in the world, just the problems I hold."

She smiled, shifted her body towards me and shook out her hands, lightly cracking the knuckles of each hand. She said, "I used to be pretty lonely; I would paint and draw at home and never go out to see other people. Then something changed in me: I wanted to learn about other people and explore their personalities and adventure with them. But I couldn't. I hadn't ever shared who I was and I was pretty bad at it at first."

"Great, it sounds like something Plath would say."

"You've read Plath?"

"It's only from her journals, but we read it in boarding school."

Her eyebrows knit together, "Do you remember what she said?"

I hesitated, then found the words sitting in my throat, "Something like, 'And when at last you find someone to whom you feel you can pour out your soul, you stop in shock at the words you utter—,'" I hesitated to look at her and continued on when I saw her eyes closed and a smile on her lips, "'they are so rusty, so ugly, so meaningless and feeble from being kept in the small cramped dark inside you so long.'"

She sighed heavily, "How did you mesmerize that so well?"

"Years of being told to memorize everything, I guess."

She said, "I learned the more you have disclosed in the past, the more likely you will easily transition into new groups. If you haven't ever shared yourself before, you won't be too good at it at first."

"Will you remember that the next time you start to think of my problems?" I asked her. "Remember that I'm new to this."

"Maybe act it. Humility is more accepted than arrogance," she said frankly.

I asked, "Is it?"

"I've learned that, too. The…" she looked up, again, towards the post office beyond the overhead railway bringing trains to and from the East Bay. She continued, "I've learned that the hard way."

"Want to tell me about the ways you've learned?" I asked.

She asked jubilantly, "Want me to show you?"

Lifting myself up with my palms against the cold steel, I thought to extend my hand out to her. She shrugged her shoulders up as a smile sprung to her face.

"You don't have to try to be amazing with me," she told me.

"I'm just trying to mirror you," I told her.

"No," she began correcting me as we descended from the boat, "you don't have to try. You just are."

We jumped over the grass of the backlot to let ourselves into the cafe through the backdoor. Before I went in, I looked at the black area where the hot coals had sucked Leonard's body into the ground, somberly. The cafe was bustling, but my eyes met Jake's quickly and I touched Cecilia's arm to point out the pair near the door.

"Well," said Jake as he reached for me when Cecilia and I had pulled away from the crowd, "would you say our work here is done?"

Ellsie was standing beside him, smiling with her arms behind her back. I stepped out of the way of a couple of cafe patrons coming or leaving. I looked between the two of them, shamelessly speechless.

"Good, then." He said, eyebrows raising, "Good." He gave me one last look.

"Listen," I began, wishing to divert the topic away from his staying in town, "about my father-"

"Everything is taken care of. I have the best doctor I know on his case."

"Really?" I asked as my peripherals caught Cecilia shifting her head to look at me fully. I turned my chin towards her and smiled with it. My mind was racing.

"We'll be leaving with him, shortly."

"You're leaving, then?" I asked looking distractedly at my aunt's dogs next to Jake's ankles.

"You're not upset about that, are you?" Ellsie asked. The drastic changes she had taken since we had exorcise Leonard were most apparent now, and I wanted to take them up with her, but my eyes hesitantly looked towards her father. I didn't want to say anything that would upset their relationship. I took her hands in mine.

"I am," I said, "But only because I will miss you two so much." I grimaced at having been so insincere with them after all they had done, but I didn't know any other way.

"As we are," Jake told me while wrapping his hug around me, "be any more like your father and you'll get yourself dead," he whispered in my ear.

I pulled away and let my elbows lock as I held his shoulders at arms length away from me. He gave me a weak smile, one that was vulnerable and sad. I could tell there were mysteries about my father and past that he could answer.

"Only you can answer the questions about your future," he intoned as he opened the door and let Ellsie slowly walk out in front of him. "Cecilia, so nice to meet you."

"Unrequited!" She giggled as she yelled after him. I looked at her sternly.

"What?" she asked, tucking the mockery behind a demure smile.

"Did your mother," I began to ask as she winced, "tell you Ellsie might be pregnant with a demi-God?" I asked.

She smirked as we walked to the line of patrons about to order, "Was that even real?"

"Are you asking or telling?" I asked.

"I guess I should tell you," she said, "it wasn't."

"I want to believe," I said.

She jabbed me, "Well I'm not doctor, but you sound like you need a skeptic by your side."

"I..." I thought about how I knew Ellsie had been having sex up there, how I had been so close to her, and felt sick. I felt violated in a way. How had that happened in a way that I could explain it to Cecilia? I had heard Ellsie scream, wished I could be there with her, and I was. But was I also inside of her? That word, I didn't want to think of that word. Inside.

How would Cecilia think about it if I didn't? I shuddered and felt a shock of something unnatural race up and down my spine until it settled, like a rat in a maze finally nibbling its cheese.

"I don't know if I feel good," I said, doubling over.

"I'm sorry," she said.

I held up a hand, "No, don't be."

She scoffed, a noise that made my stomach lurch even more, and she said, "It's a reflexive action to apologize, but I guess I'm not sorry."

"Want to go for a drive?" I asked.

She smiled out of the corner of her mouth and her eyes bunched up, "Of course."

I wished I could have looked at her longer. I wished we weren't already moving. I wished we could have stopped to sit across from one another, watching each other instead of watching the road. I could watch the light move around her while she remained flawless. I would have forgotten to eat or breathe. I would have forgotten that she needed to eat and move. I would have destroyed us both if I had done that, but I still wish I had. Instead, we were moving very fast and I thought only for a second to look at her again, before I had to look away, to only think very quickly but very deeply about the beautiful person she was.

I could not stop for long. She pulled back her hair and looked up to me, to register my intent gaze, maybe. Maybe she was trying to ask me why I had stopped with her eyes. Or maybe she was slowly mustering the courage to speak a word of love. Or maybe she was simply happier or appreciating some unknown thing. I hope she saw how I appreciated her and I hope she was happier for it.

She directed my hands with her words as the amber glow from the lights on 7th St. We were going towards the part of Oakland that had a bigger city feel. It was less of a community and more of an economy there, but she had me turn left off of 7th before we had gotten out of the projects. The biggest buildings were community houses and government-sponsored buildings that brought in no revenue, just offered housing. I parked the car away from our destination, which seemed to be a nondescript area on Adeline St.

Cecilia turned her body in her seat to face me, which I always liked. I detested the way two people in a car would face away from one another while trying to enjoy one another.I smiled at her, trying to show her my gratitude to see her and have her face me.

She looked back at me, "What happens here is not for you to share," she said resolutely. I asked her to give me a reason and I watched as her dark eyes started to work. They moved sideways and I thought I'd lost her when they bounced back, only to slide sideways again.

I had seen this movement of eyes before and I knew that she was writing and putting down in hundreds of words why, but all she said was, "Reasons," as her eyes slid across her page of mind once more, "many of them."

She and I walked south down the street. She adjusted her black hair to shield her face and approached an electronic road sign that read, MERGE AHEAD KEEP LEFT.

"Look out for me," she yelled as she crouched next to the orange base. It was flanked by orange safety cones and had two wheels on either side of the large box. In the middle was a vertical orange pole holding the electric panel up. Cecilia flipped open a piece of metal on the orange base.

"They generally have a small lock on them, not this time," she said slyly.

I nodded, watching a car pass.

"This is the access panel," she said, then picked up a big black object that looked like a geometry calculator attached to a curly black cord, "Well, it's asking me for a

152

password and I don't have one for it. How about I…" she pressed two fingers onto the pad. "Control, shift…D-I-P-Y," she muttered, almost to herself. "Dots!" she said while shaking out her hair and letting it fall against her knees. I crouched down next to her and could tell that the smell of her hair was strong over the smell of warm tires and old tarmac.

"You've done this before or just now find out how to do this?" I asked as a duo of headlights illuminated the both of us and passed.

"Remember when I said I wanted to show you my world?" she asked.

"I do," I said.

"Well, this," she said while typing, "is it!"

She returned the black control pad to the panel and closed the lid on it. She looked up at me and smiled while she took a lock out of her purse. The metal glinted lightly as she hooked it around the panel and tore the key from it.

"So they can't change it." She said with a smile, "Even if I can."

Her hands were in her pockets and she had turned from the road sign and me. I hooked my neck to look up at the sign, which now read THE ONLY THING YOU SHOULD TAKE IS TIME.

We both walked casually fast back to my car. I started the engine, the noise of it becoming a cacophony of tempos and sounds that matched the twitching flutters of my very own heart, which I could feel beat an unsteady rhythm.

I looked at Cecilia next to me, quickly, as I drove. Her chest pushed against her bundle of black curls and I could see her breathing quickly as she looked around, then to me. Sadly, I turned my eyes away from her. If those moments in life, where I had to turn away from the things I loved, if those moments could be stilled.

Or forgotten.

Or gone.

If, then.

I would be a happier man, now.

I would not look back with regret.

I would know, now, that I had watched it all. I had missed nothing. There was no mistaking it, I had lived to the fullest.

But the man I am now, looking back and remembering her giddy smile, regrets ever looking away from it.

This man remembering her now wants to know if she regrets anything, or if she blames me for looking away.

Then, when both of our hearts were like untamed animals caged by our own ribs, she could not hold my eyes but held my hand. She loosened it as I had to use mine to shift. It tightened on the straight-aways when I didn't have to. When the engine slowed and she could hear there was an imminent shift, she loosened her grip and her hand hovered over mine as it moved.

When I thought to ask where she wanted to go, when I looked over with my mouth agape, about to ask what she wanted to do, she pushed her black eyebrows down and a small smile sprung up, then fell again. I didn't ask where to go. I just went where my feet and hands could take us on the gas and wheel.

We went past the small skyscrapers of Oakland's downtown. We saw graffiti from deadeyes, and, of course, old crow, and gats streak by our window too fast for me to really appreciate. I smiled out of the corner of my mouth, thinking that Cecilia probably knew the artists, or had already stood next to the red-brick walls and freeway overpasses to look up at the painted portraits of their perspectives.

I said her name, "Cecilia," and realized it was like a sigh I had held in for months. I took another breath in, worried about the words that were gone and that only her name filled my mouth. "Cecilia."

She did not expect a return word, but turned her body to me in her seat and let the side of her head rest against the headrest. I glanced to see her thick lashes close over her eyes as her hand lifted up and held mine again. I shifted the car with my left hand instead of the hand she held for a few minutes. Eventually, she began to loosen her hand when I needed to move mine to change gears. In her lazy lean against the seat, she made an effort to hear the roars and whines of the engine and predict when I would need my hand to shift. I held my breath behind a smile.

I sighed again and realized, the only way I remembered to breathe was to say her name. "Cecilia."

I say it hundred dozen times to myself before we move into the Berkeley streets, like a cat slinking into a neighborhood it once knew, I drove us in. Her eyelashes fluttered as I drove. Lights bounced from the lit lamps to the slick street, then bounced back to the lights. They shone twice as bright as they would have if they had nothing to fall on. My eyes fell on her, and they shone twice as bright than if there had been nothing.

When we stopped, I exhaled slowly after turning off the engine, thankful for every breath next to her. I looked over as she moved, her hand moved to my shoulder, her seatbelt un-clicked and she pushed herself towards me. My mouth was warm and wet with her. I thought about how often it was only our own mouth we tasted. Besides food and drink, that is almost only what we tasted. Except, of course, when we got to overturn that routine and taste one another.

When we got out of the car, the sky was bright with the stars the universe was breathing out on us. If it had been asked of me, I would have said that the sun went around the earth in the same way that my mind wrapped around Cecilia. I would have said tectonic plates shifted to make room for her and volcanoes erupted because she put pressure on the Earth to be as hot as her.

Outside, she came to my side of the car quickly and opened the door for me, like a gentleman. I unfurled my legs like a scroll full of long-forgotten words falling open and spilling to the pebble-strewn asphalt. I coaxed a smile to my face to hide my anxiety at my inability to stand. I wondered if I would be able to speak any words with her name so close to the back of my teeth. She shut the door for me and held both her hands over one of mine.

"This over here looks a bit like an alley you might see in Europe," she said, looking longingly at the stone-walled passageway behind her.

I willed words for her and they came slowly, "Do you want to go down there or up to the top?"

Her eyes brightened, "To the top of where?"

"To the top," I reiterated while smiling and grabbing her hand. We walked up the trail, pointing out the plants, city lights, and silhouettes. Her feet stumbled and I did not waver in enveloping her body in mine before it could fall. Our embraces were not gentle and short, as together we were nubile and naive to the contours of one another.

I ran my fingers along the lines of her muscles and ligaments and bones, like chalk on butcher paper reading raised hieroglyphic relief works. Like those ancient inscriptions, I could not have read the story that each line and contour told. Were the dimples on her shoulders from climbing a bunk-bed and getting strong, from using an axe and cutting wood, from rowing a boat, or just in her genetics? Were the furrows on the bottom of her forearms from drawing or writing? Were there sad stories to go along with her scars that I would listen to, memorize, and learn to empathize with or were they ones even she didn't remember anymore?

She pushed back my hair, suckled on my ear, and breathed into it longing without words. When we could, we took in our views. To the West, we could see both the East Bay and San Francisco. When we looked to the East, we saw great redwood arrows jutting from the horizon. Box-like houses were shrouded by trees on their curving streets underneath us on the university side of Berkeley, while beyond that the industrious buildings and warehouses of Oakland's linear streets spread out until they were cut off by the bay's water, which twinkled and picked up light from the cities surrounding it. From West Oakland, a bridge curved out, into Treasure Island, a small island made of trees, trash, and small levels of radiation, then curved again, this time, to the left to go towards San Francisco.

I remembered landing there by airplane and looking down at the sweeping valleys and rivers of light that laid on the city. It was enough to make me wonder if the two sets of a dozen ribs each was enough to hold my organs intact when a system so planned and formidable was able to deteriorate, too.

I looked over at Cecilia, rubbed her shoulder, and kissed the only part of her hair that was straight, the roots.She looked up at me and pushed a kiss from her mouth to my nose.

That night, we slept on her porch and did not wake up to pick figs nor push our bodies into one another. We slept in order to hold one another close.

Chapter Nine

In the morning, while Cecilia was showering and readying herself, Edna and I sat and had what she called Spanish-style coffee in the backyard. She had already fed her goats and chickens and they touched the ground with their velvet lips or marble-hard beaks, curious about where more food could possibly be. The coffee was thick and grainy, but did the trick well and my lips were loosened by it.

I had been itching to ask her, "You said that we were far from the Hanging Gardens," I said, "when we were dealing with Leonard Kiljun."

"I said that of Babylon, yes." She replied coolly, "I was referring to my gardens here, which are nestled in a metropolis much like Babylon."

I asked, "How are they like it?"

"Do you know much about Babylon?" she asked.

I shook my head, no.

"You probably don't know because nobody likes to talk about past mistakes." She began, "But there are always parts of history that you can relate to the present. I, personally, see two things about the past and present that can be talked about quickly. A weak tribe from

Media conquered Babylon according to prediction and a large number of Jewish people were exiled there, in Babylon. There were once beautiful hanging gardens, like the ones behind my house, as well as amazing temples and pyramid-like structures. That is where the gardens were. Not on the ground but raised. Jewish people have not been exiled to Oakland, but, you know that Latino families have been, as well as the overwhelming number of black people forced out and then back in, you know." She trailed off with her eyes to the yellow flowers dangling from their vines.

I nodded my head formally, then said, "Is it like the Museum at Halicarnassus, Lighthouse of Alexzandria, Colossus of Rhodes, Temple of Artemis at Ephesus?"

She smiled, "Smart boy, yes. It was one of the wonders. Why don't you ask about Pyramid of Giza?"

"It isn't one of the destroyed ones."

"Then how do you know any of those previous ones have existed at all?" She asked.

"Because I have already been to the Babylonian gardens in your backyard," I said with a smile and a tip of my coffee cup into my mouth.

She said, "The rest are fiction to go to now, in a different part of history."

"Are they really? What if they exist but have not been examined?" I said.

"I think what some people might call you is a conspiracy theorist, but I understand. Only the tip of the iceberg has been touched by human examination."

"I'm a theorist, but I don't tip into conspiracy. Not unless I want to believe the lies I can tell myself to account for the lies of others. Tell me, why do you think Babylon is here?"

She strung together words with her fingers as she said, "Today, the same has been done as far as exile goes. A large number of minority individuals have been detained in Oakland and any other area where the majority finds unsuitable living conditions. Then people are forced there. Once inside, they are not given proper care, are forced into servitude to systems not their own, and their cultures become constrained. Plus, I have hanging gardens."

I thought about Edna's common struggle with her neighbors to keep her home, garden, and block a friendly and habitable place. It wasn't easy when the trash from three different cities seemed to find its way to your doorstep and the collectors in the green city trucks found a dump not a hundred feet from your house.

"Ironically enough, a different kind of media has ruined it." She looked down, at her leathery brown hands and closed her eyes, breathing in and out deeply.

I nodded again and sipped my coffee slowly, distancing myself from words at the back of my throat that I didn't understand.

She finally spoke again, "Women and men and children are upset and angry, but the media calls their genuine indignation at oppression 'drama' and calls the shutting down of the systems that help them 'politics,' which is disgusting and wrong. When will they see that it is the inability to have basic empathy; that is not politics."

"And because people see that," I began to say.

"They think they better act on what they're told- if they're imbeciles, yes. How many white men have killed little black boys lately?" she asked me, "How many times has a little boy of color like you been treated as a problem, without anybody seeing that the world he is growing up in is the one with the problems? There is legitimate anger at the allocation of human rights, but what is there to do?"

"Remaining angry does little," I said.

She sang softly to herself and stated, "When I'm angry I hum or sing. What do you do?"

I said, "I count."

"Oh?" She giggled at me.

"Yeah, I let everything go from my mind and I just start counting before I can think anything else that I don't want to think. I don't set a goal or think too much about what number I am on." I told her, "I just count and count and count until I feel calm enough to think again."

"That is most certainly meditation," she told me as she rung a bell, picked up a crystal, then lit a small piece of perfectly fine wood on fire.

"San Pedro," she said, holding up the wood.

"What?"

"The name of this wood," she said and I could smell the musty, sweet scent of it. It was like smelling baked goods in the middle of the forest. It was an intoxicating smell. She gazed at the yellow bell-shaped flower hanging from the short tree.

"Smells nice," I said.

"Angel's trumpets, Hell's bells, Brugmansia" she said with a look of pain on her face.

"I am sorry, what?" I asked.

The smile flickered back to her lips as she looked at me again, "The many names of those flowers."

"Oh," I said, unable to register their importance then.

"Brugmansia," she drawled out the name. "Very good for-" she paused, looking at me concernedly, then said, "-you know. Either that or you don't want to know."

I shook my head, "I think it's simpler than that."

"Few things in life are," she said. "Let me tell you a secret," she said, hushedly, "Cecilia is a color girl."

"Huh?" I asked, feeling heat rising to my face as I thought of all of the consequences of reacting too quickly. I asked as my eyes moved like I was watching a bird crossing my vision. I thought quickly, trying to understand what she was saying about me. Was she insulting me? Was she happy Cecilia was with a boy with my race? Should I be at least thankful she was accepting or resentful that she was pointing a finger?

"She likes to breathe in her favorite color. She really lets her entire body fill up with it and breathes out the one she likes least." I breathed a sigh of relief as she explained, "Works for her quite well as a meditative tactic."

"She's a color girl when she meditates, I get it." I nodded vaguely, wondering when I could have used that to help her in the past.

"Here she is," Edna said as Cecilia descended down the stairs.

"What were you talking about?" Cecilia asked as she removed her phone from her backpack, checking it with her face turned downward.

"Self-preservation," Edna stated.

Cecilia gripped her bottom lip in-between her teeth and nodded slightly, "Well, we were going to go."

"Right," I said, smiling at Edna and picking myself up from the warmth of the bench and the garden, leaving the warmth and security of a mother's presence for that of Oakland's streets.

She walked fast, her boots hitting the ground hard and her chin almost pressed against the top of her chest.

"What's wrong?" I asked.

She shook her head, "Nothing at all."

"I'll be patient." I said as I walked with her, almost chasing after her.

"I know you won't be."

"Do you?" I asked.

"Well," she said, almost starting a sentence.

"I'll be patient," I repeated.

Cecilia spoke softly, "She was really emotionally abusive," and slowly.

"Was she? She seems so much different than all that," I said.

She looked at me as we walked, her deep brown eyes had blue flowers blossom around the irises. I realized tears were forming. I thought about how I knew nothing about other people.

"All I've ever wanted is for my parents," I almost said more, but I had nothing else to say. I had always only wanted them. "I guess I don't understand what it's like to have a parent do something wrong."

"To some degree, she is not to blame. She didn't know. She would hurt me with something she'd say and I would let her know that I was upset, but she would then use that hurt and pain against me, too," she explained softly as she pressed only one foot into each square of cement in the sidewalk. "All of a sudden I was doing something that hurt her when I was hurt, and I would have to apologize."

I bit my lip, knowing I couldn't say the right thing, knowing to only say she did not have to be alone. "I'm here for you," I said.

"I'm here for myself. Nobody else has picked me up the way that I can," she said.

I wanted to remove my hand from her waist, take my body away from hers, watch her from a distance that wouldn't scare her, but I also wanted to let her stay in control. I would not leave unless she asked. I wanted her to know I would be there, but only if that was what she wanted.

"And all of a sudden, my emotions are invalid and my words are silenced and," she began to touch the tracks the tears left on her cheeks. I pushed my thumb against them before the wind could make her face cold.

"All of a sudden," she began again, "I'm damaged and I don't want others to have anything to do with my feelings. I don't know when they'll be used against me, again."

"At least you understand it all." I mused, "That awareness will help you get over it."

She laughed, "If I can articulate why I am a victim, I am not seen as a victim anymore."

"I love you very much for being such a strong person now. For being who you are now took time and trouble and-"

She interrupted me, "I just want you to know why I might be closed. Why I might be cold. But I won't play games with you. I don't want to knock down your queen with my bishop, take all your cards, or end your happiness."

"I want you to enjoy being with me," I said.

"I want it for you, now, just as much as I want it for myself."

"Cecilia," I said, simply, "I wish more people were like you. You're honest and genuine and care enough about yourself to care about others. You may just be my favorite person in all of the world."

"Do you know what it feels like," she started to ask, "to have somebody say your name while looking you in the eyes the entire time?"

I wanted to say nothing more that could ruin the look of approval on her face.

"Ryan," she said while holding my gaze, "it feels amazing being with you."

"Get down!" I heard.

I saw her eyes, little orbs conveying worry and fear.

I saw my hands against her head, pulling and pushing her to the ground.

If somebody yelled at us to get down or if I thought it, I do not know, but I heard it and I was covering Cecilia's bundles of curls and face while I pressed my torso and legs into the ground.

"Stay down!" Men with darting eyes and handguns moved past us. One watched me watching them. He was unarmed, wearing a knit gray scarf and a puffy black jacket. Dazedly, I felt like I had seen him in my dad's house. I had seen him in one of the photographs.

"Him!" he said, gesturing with his jaw as he licked his lips. He ducked his head as another man opened a Suburban's door for him. I looked to the license plate before looking up at the man approaching me. His right hand swept behind his head and whipped back towards me. I removed myself from his hand's path, knocking my head against the cement as I dodged.

He sneered, "Like that?"

I asked, "What do you want?"

"Come on!" Came a yell from the Suburban.

The man in front of me shook his head, hazel eyes shining as they reflected the gray of the morning sky. I shook my head at him as I realized in his right hand was a gun. I tried to put away the notion that he was going to merely club me with it. Was he going to leave now or make it worse?

Would a fool wait for him to react? Would a fool react too quickly? I asked myself. He pointed his gun, I grabbed his wrist and turned it up. His mouth opened and his grip grew soft.

"No!" came a voice in my head, "Do not meddle with the four!" It was not the voice I usually hear when I think. It was louder. The voice in my head is not always my own, but it always the same volume. This voice was so loud it hurt to hear.

I shook my head, trying to control my own thoughts, and in doing so lost control of my hands. The man realized my grip had softened and pushed the gun forward, hitting me directly in my right temple. I watched him walk away from my view on the ground.

The suburban sucked rocks around the tires and spat them out as it drove away. My view of it, and the entire street, darkened.

I was licking a pine tree.

Chapter Ten

No, no I was not.

"What is that?" I heard myself say incoherently.

"Gin," Cecilia's voice came back to me.

"Don't ever do that to me," I told her.

"Come on, we have to get off the street," she said to me. She pocketed her brushed steel flask.

I asked sloppily, "Why?"

"Because we're going to get shot!"

That is enough for anybody to know to listen. We were closer to the cafe than her house. For a moment I thought we could break into the house I was going to ask her to move into with me, but I liked the idea of a surprise that did not mask an original, and maybe more deadly, surprise. We ran to the cafe and when we had closed the glass door behind us, we breathed strongly, sighing and smiling, and inevitably giggling into one another's shoulders as we sighed anxieties.

Cecilia shook her head, "We just-"

I put a hand on Cecilia's chest and looked at her, "I would say your heart is the one about the do the shooting."

"So happy you both saw what we all did," Tre said from a chair near us.

I stood up a little taller, "What was that?"

"Well," he began as he stood and put both of his hands on our shoulders, "you two were doing this sort of flirting where apparently neither of you knew you were flirting, but everybody else did."

Cecilia and I must have mirrored one another's half-smiles. What a good opportunity to be reminded of what we had both been hoping for so long.

"You're very insightful today," I said.

"Oh yes, " he said, cocking his head. "Also, an octopus is just a wet spider."

"Thanks for that," Cecilia said, showing both sets of teeth as she winced.

"Hey mcnuggs, I hope you're having as terrible of a day as I am," said the surly barista. I noticed how her eyelids didn't move up or down much at all when she talked, unless it was about a boyfriend or a new tattoo.

"When people treat you like they don't care," I began, "believe them."

"Who asked me to care? I don't need to care about you to take your order and let you bum cigarettes off me."

Cecilia smiled, "Hi, how are you today?"

"Terrible. Just awful." She smiled, happy for something that I didn't understand.

"I think bakers," Tre began, "should ask egg farmers about counting." He raised his top lip in a Billy Idol-esque grin and nodded his head at her.

"That isn't something to really consider," she started in, inhaling to begin a diatribe against his imbecility, but he began talking again.

"Can I get a," he inhaled and she looked expectant, almost happy to just be taking an order, "what-what?"

She puckered her lips together, "I do not have to serve you, especially if you're making bad jokes," and started frantically hitting her fist against the tile counter.

Cecilia put her hand on her wrist and I asked her, "I don't think I've ever asked you your name."

"It's Zierra." She looked at me squarely, willing me to remember, "With a Z."

"Really?" I said, "Well Zierra I'd like some coffees for all of three of us and two breakfast sandwiches. Whatever you already have out works for the meat, bread, and cheese." I dropped a twenty onto the counter and placed my hand on Tre's back, "How about you sit down outside?"

He turned to walk outside, but yelled over his shoulder, presumably to Zierra, "It's easier to be angry at someone then to tell them they're hurt!" Cecilia and I turned towards each other and smiled. Were we smiling because it was melodramatic or because it was information we both needed, I don't know.

"Wow. Some people," Zierra said gruffly while sweeping the bill into the drawer and handing us three mugs.

I said, "Keep the change, thanks." I smiled again at Cecilia and turned around.

Sol was standing there, key dangling above her head. She held it between her thumb and forefinger, grinning widely, "I heard that this is rightfully yours now!"

"Thanks!" I said, as I pulled it into my pocket. "Can I have copies made?"

I could tell this was not going to be a short conversation when Sol dramatically cocked her head to the side and put her hand under her head in thought. Cecilia kissed my ear and nodded a goodbye to Sol as she moved towards the cafe's wet-bar.

"Sure!" Sol said, "I have never known him to do this, just let you stay there! It must be less nice inside than your last place!"

"Well, I am fixing it up," I said.

"But really," she said as we moved out of the walkway for other patrons, "How did you do it? This guy doesn't often do nice things." She began, pulling me close to her, "You know me, I am all about the community. I'll lay myself on the bare ground for it! But this guy, not the same way. You know, it takes all kinds of people to really form a village. He's just another piece of the puzzle. I feel like we do have that here in West Oakland."

"Sol," I said, thinking I would start to tell her about what Cecilia and I had just run away from, "There are still some darker deeds going on and I value what you can do."

"Do you think I can fix the community? I do everyday. I have a lot of obligations to it, but so do you."

I stuttered, "Normative values are the source of obligations."

She said, "Do you have enough of those values to make it? We almost always have a chance to gain new beliefs and learn."

"But values are separate from beliefs," I said, calculating how much I should bring up. My mind became muddled with both worry and relief about what I wanted to tell about my cousins and Leonard, maybe because it seemed a simpler story.

She said, "I value you. This is neither true nor false. You are true."

"Right you are."

"What do you value? It isn't true nor false, in any case, but it is interesting."

"I can't stop thinking about Leonard Kiljun," I admitted to Sol. He was gone, but so were they. There was the sweet sorrow in it. The spirituality Edna brought into it diffused what had happened, what I had felt.

"But, really, the violence does not always have to be here." She interjected after musing on what she said, "The crime here is mostly to do with the drug users and young homeless kids. Did you know that our first mayor of Oakland was once one of those squatters, in his day! Did you know that?" she had a habit of tugging on my elbow when talking, "Just look at our walls, they are so much more colorful on every single street, every single day. There is more art on one street in Oakland than ten in the city next to us- not to put it down." She said with a hushed voice, "There's nothing too flashy about West Oakland, but we have something good going. We do."

I thought of where the crime used to be and where it was going. I thought about whoI was if I thought I could do this. I fought back the shame with what I knew.

I realized I shouldn't be tangential in the dialogue with Sol about crime and that nothing I was thinking would be pertinent, so asked, instead, "What if somebody bigger than just your everyday drug-user or homeless kid was a criminal." I asked, "What if there was more organized crime here?"

She laughed, "Well I don't want to say I would appreciate it," I tilted my head to show her my ear was listening to her speak, "but it's better than small crime in my eyes. When there is big crime the small criminals don't really have a place to fit into it."

I chose to advocate both sides and said, "What negative affects can be seen?"

"Big crime can hurt the entire community where it is weak," she thought again for a moment's breath, "but big criminals usually target the smaller ones and," she gulped, "they get rid of them," and nodded, "and big crime becomes the entire neighborhood's enemy. This neighborhood loves itself," she said, "it will never think that way."

"Smaller criminals won't get sucked up into it?" I asked, worrying about kids on the street and people that were new to the game joining.

"Like I said, this neighborhood loves itself. It won't let that happen. It wants to see its kids succeed so much, every single person in it will point their fingers at the real bad guys and stigmatize them so much, the kids won't touch them. They won't touch them." She backed off of me a little, letting me breathe.

I thought about the man who was flipping though the bags of my stuff on the porch telling me to have a nice day. I thought about Charles in his wheelchair, kindly offering me his gift for gab in exchange for a more pleasant day. I thought about a dozen times I had seen pure love coming from people here and being given by me for them.

"It does," I said.

She nodded and licked her lips to continue talking, "And so it will heal itself if it needs to."

"It will," I agreed.

"With or without your help," she said, raising her eyebrows above her sunglasses quite a bit.

"Who wants my help, really?" I asked.

She looked me up and down, "Well what am I doing?"

I chuckled, "Letting me help."

She grabbed my collarbone and said vehemently, "Exactly. Your voice can always be heard. Your ability to take a step towards change is what makes the change. It isn't a war that starts a revolution, it is a simple shift," she snapped her fingers, "in mindset."

I began to amble away when she said, "One last thing." I turned and she said, "In the back lot," I nodded, knowing it well already, "we have a garden going and Artie said what with you living so close…" she let her words trail off.

"I would love to help." I laughed, "You know that."

She nodded approvingly, "Anything you can do."

"I'll put my hands in the dirt."

Sol gripped my collarbone again as she pulled me in for a hug, "I love you like I love my family. Your family is not necessarily where you keep your blood but where your heart feels strongest."

I smiled, softly letting memories of Cecilia, Sol, Charles, Edna, Ellsie, all of them, wash over me.

I ambled again, letting my heels press into the ground slowly as I thought. I found myself thinking of all of the ways I found myself able to contribute, and in doing so thought of all of the things I was good at.

Funny that I had never listed my positive traits in my head. I stirred cream and sugar into my coffee remotely detached from my hands and arms. I thought more about the slow process it had been from growing up in a boarding school where I was completely unaware of my parents. I didn't know if they were the people who loved me enough to put my safety over everything else. I was happy to be myself when I thought about that; only recently did I know that they existed and that I wasn't so alone. Before, I had been strong enough to let myself rely on no man other than myself. Now, I was strong enough to let my dad rely on me. I sipped the coffee, feeling warmer and stronger from it.

I walked to the back patio after picking up the sandwiches from the barista, who slid them across the countertop unenthusiastically and began to berate her newest patrons for referring to the menu.

"Do you even come here?" I heard her ask.

"Yes, I do!"

"Then list five of our menu items, right now. Without looking at the menu," she said to him while her entire face and body was set in a stoic and aggressive position.

The patron stuttered and looked around confusedly. I wanted to give him a consoling gesture, but was on the side of the distributor in order to avoid hostile relations in the future.

In the back, Cecilia was eyeing Tre and a few other guys in a similar manner. She didn't shift her gaze too much when I opened the door, intent on what they were saying.

"Tell me," she said, rolling her hand in front of her. I set her plate in front of her.

"I just think," Tre began lamely, "that women should be taught while they are girls," he moved his hands like he was shuffling furniture, "not to hit boys."

"You have to be taught not to hit me," Cecilia rolled her eyes and shook out one side of her hair with her hand, "because I can't hurt you as well when I hit you."

"I may be wrong," Tre said, "I think I am wrong based on the number of times that a woman's attacked me, unprovoked."

Cecilia cleared her throat, then said, "How can women assume men won't hurt them when statistically women are more likely to be hurt by a man than live the rest of their lives happily together. It is completely and totally appropriate. Margarat Atwood found that women are afraid of being hurt or killed by men whereas men fear being embarrassed by them."

We all looked at her, open-mouthed.

She asked us, "Do any of you find that ridiculous?"

Tre and I looked at one another and I said, "Only shocked that men can be narrow-minded enough to not see the obvious problem there."

Tre said, "I feel guilty for ever being afraid of a girl making me feel bad when," he slowed his speech, "they get actually hurt, hurt," he drew out the word, "I forgot that that is a legitimate fear."

"Now you're getting it," Cecilia said.

Tre looked at her and said, "I don't know what I could have done wrong like those men that I don't want to be, though."

"Tre," Cecilia asked, "What made this girl hit you?"

"Huh?" he asked, looking very vulnerable.

Cecilia asked again.

"I told you I didn't provoke her," he said.

"Oh?" she said, as I nodded towards one of the guys cigarette packs and bummed one off of him.

"I told her I wanted to," he said while nodding slowly and looking down. Cecilia gave him a scorning look. He retracted his words with a flail of hands.

He started again, "And she didn't want to. So, I, well, I had gotten worked up down there and I may have said that I was going to leave. Just for the night, but I needed to go blow off steam after seeing her get all sexy and undressed and in bed."

"Do you want to get to know this woman?" Cecilia asked while throwing her hands in her lap.

"Of course." Tre said, clasping his hands, "I was on my hands and knees begging her to date me four months ago. I want to know her in and out."

"A woman is not written in braille." Cecilia said sternly. "You do not need to touch her to get to know her. You know I heard that once and never thought I would be saying it?"

"Ryan," she said my name harshly and I looked up, "is this the kind of thing I would ever have to tell you?"

"Me?" I asked, quizzing myself on everything we had done. I thought of my favorite color, a few lines of Shakespeare, and the shape of a ball of rubber bands. I did not know what to answer.

"No, me. Am I the type of girl that needs to say no a billion different ways? No. But this girl might be. This girl might be sensitive. This girl might have had a man rub her the wrong way without asking and now she needs to rest it up down there or little tears come out. You understand, Tre?"

He shook his head, eyebrows forcing new frown lines into his forehead.

"Do you know what kind of culture we live in?" Cecilia asked.

Tre looked around doubtfully.

"Do you know what kind of culture we live in?" She asked again.

"A rape culture," said one of the men sitting near us.

Cecilia nodded and put a hand in the air. "Yes, a culture where girls are asked what they did to make men hit or rape them. One where women go out with their friends in groups, in part, to avoid predatory men. Then men make fun of them for having to always go out with their friends in packs." Tre nodded, letting his frown fall down against his chin, "Where women have clues and signals to let their friends know that they are becoming victimized by a predatory man. We are in a culture that does not tell a girl that it isn't her fault for being raped. We live in a culture that tells them in every conceivable way that they did something wrong, that we triggered a man to do what he did." She took a drink of coffee, but none of us thought for a moment that we should contribute to the conversation.

She continued, "So I am sorry if women have shown you that they get triggered easily, too, but we are being defensive and we aren't putting up with predators amongst humans. And, yes, maybe mamas and papas should start telling their little girls that violence is not okay from them nor to them, but right now teaching little boys that violence is not okay is a big challenge, am I right?"

We all nodded, thinking about our own obligation to women. I thought not about the things that most people had taught me about violence, but about my own desires, emotions, and lack of control. Violent video games, media, and movies had not taught me to resort to violence. The way that it was the only outlet presented yo me was the reason. I thought about the sensitivities I may have lacked to see in women and girls if I made them hurt or feel uncomfortable.

"One last thing," she said with a finger in the air, "when you make assumptions, you limit your sensitivities. Alright, I'm done." She ate a piece of meat from the breakfast sandwich.

"Hi," said the man sitting near us. "Scuba Steve here and I just want to say that I have officially gotten rid of all assumptions and opinions I have about women. I'm done and dumb." He shook her hand and she smiled while wiping something from the corner of her mouth. He was a stalky, pink man with pants torn at the thighs and his messenger bag still slung over his back. His mouth seemed to be perpetually open, showing his four front teeth, and he had pale blue eyes. Next to him sat a quite, olive-skinned man with a comb-over that remained silent.

"Thank you," she said, "I don't know. We shouldn't be sitting around here in this day and age talking like this." She shrugged then looked at Tre, "I still think you have a point, it's just that there are other lessons to be learned before that point makes sense. It's like, we -as humans, not just you and me- have barely gotten past this one step towards equality that we can't jump ahead."

Scuba Steve shrugged, "We're all humanitarians, aren't we?"

She nodded her entire body forward, "Yeah. We are." She looked around herself, at the pail furniture and silly artwork, then said, "We should be."

I was floored. I had been repressed. I had never breathed a breath thinking so much outside of myself. I wanted to whisper positive affirmations in Cecilia's ear for an eternity of moments, but I also thought that that may be an invasion of personal space. That may be exactly what she was saying should not happen.

I felt the great many places inside myself that I held my thoughts and ideas emptied. The vessels that had once contained so much merely had lines along the wall, marking where the contents had grown in colorful colors. I closed my eyes and looked in on those places, feeling deliberately hollow. I looked at those places and wondered if I would fill them up just as deliberately as I planned. I might just fail. I might fill these empty parts of my mind and body and soul with thoughts and ideas that were just as naive and miscalculated as the ones that had been there before, but I could appreciate that I had tried. That I had been able to feel this naive and new and ready for growth was both enough and not enough. Both an energizing and draining feeling. I had nothing to control and therefore had to use all of the best control.

I looked over at Cecilia, smiling in the late autumn day's sunlight as it touched both of our faces. Parts of her black hair shown white. An earring sparkled in the sun and she smirked, pulling a few ringlets of hair behind her ear as she looked at me.

"Boy," said Tre, "I sure do enjoy watching sports. When they throw the ball? The best." He smiled cheekily, and I knew he was making a joke, but it made me uncomfortable how much he was playing a role that Cecilia had just denounced. She didn't look visibly upset, but rather was laughing a bit. I looked at him condescendingly.

Tre coughed into his hand and spoke again, "If you ever need to make a meal, just put an egg in the ground. Doesn't even need to grow, it's already an eggplant!" He laughed to himself while shaking his head and I stood up, brushing the crumbs off of my pants.

"This girl you're dating, Tre," I said to him.

"Yeah?" He asked.

"See what she's doing today. Take her for a boat ride on the lake or something."

"She does love the lake." He mused, "But girls are so confusing."

Cecilia tilted her head as she stood up, "No girl that likes you wants you to be confused. She wants you to be just as happy as she is. Go show her that award-winning grin." He did smile big when she said that.

"I never do make the same mistake twice," he sighed, "I make it five or six times and then I get it right."

Cecilia cocked her head at him, then me, and we both waved good-bye to Scuba Steve and the guy sitting with us.

"So what's this about the key and Sol?" Cecilia asked me as we closed the door.

"Give me a second," I said, as I walked into the bathroom and closed the door, locking it. It was a grunge-punk bathroom that nobody would spend excess amounts of time in. I did my business quickly and I popped my head out of it and ran through the cafe to catch up with Cecilia, waving to a group of people I knew.

"Let's go see," I said to her as I caught up with her. "It is a surprise I think you will like, but who knows. Tell me, do you like living with your mom?" I asked.

She whined and shifted her body around as she kicked at the cement, "You got me there."

"Let's keep walking, then," I said.

"What is it about the human touch," I asked her as we kicked rocks on our short walk, "that stabilizes people?"

She held my hand and said, "I think it's the feeling we get of being comforted. It isn't something society has taught us, it isn't something that has been pushed into our minds, no matter how much I'd like to think it is."

"I'm thinking of the way all animals need that support at some point in their life. Is it the warmth?" I started to ask, "Is it the heartbeat, or is there something else entirely?"

"You think of it as a very physiological thing," she said, "whereas I think of it as an emotion-based one."

Our palms pressed delicately into one another and I thought of the feeling of my head against a chest, feeling the pulse of life. I thought about the first time I was touched; it was not too long ago that that happened. Of course, I had been touched when I was born and growing up, but as an adult to be touched is a very different experience. To be touched irregularly is its own realm of new and weird. It had been mystifying. My entire body stopped responding, didn't give signals to my mind or mouth. It paused. My body. My world. It had all become different. It had all made less sense. I was immediately made aware of my self-containment. Stuck inside my own body without being able to make it happier. I thought of that electric feeling that I had never gotten from professors or friends as their hands brushed against mine, gripped my shoulder, or patted my back.

We rounded the corner of the street I had been on yesterday. The street with the house where I would like to let her live with me.

She did not seem astonished as I opened the gate, nor when I unlocked the door. I thought a peculiar grin would etch on one side of her face when she saw me pick up my bag and hold it high, next to my shoulder, as I myself grinned wide. Instead, she asked me what the Grim Reaper would do if he was forced to help a woman give birth.

I laughed, "Tell her it isn't his job."

"It's the exact opposite of his job," She said, with eyes only trained on me. She was facing away from the front room and the living room and the soft lights from both rooms backlit her silhouette perfectly.

"What do you think about living here?" I asked her.

She tucked a smile under her nose and I faintly remembered the screams, screeches of railway cars and people around me, laughing as their legs and back pressed hard against metal. They were the sounds of living houseless. The noises I remembered made me think of the railway cops, called bull, because they only brought bull into your life if they caught you. Had I gotten out of the lifestyle quickly enough to be able to wash it off in a hot shower of a home or would it always be embedded in my pores? Letting go was like losing a tooth as a child; I still ran my tongue over the void for a while in shock before something could grow in its place.

"For you?" She asked timidly.

"Well," I started to say before I noticed that I was changing my tone and pitch to more easily persuade her. I looked down and around, anywhere but at her.

"For both of us," I said.

She looked like she was chewing a piece of her cheek, "Let's be like internet explorer."

I had felt like an anvil had hit my stomach, but I still didn't understand what had been said at all.

Her head bobbed and swayed like a balloon in the air, "Let's take things slow."

I felt the emotional pain activate my autonomic nervous system. In just a few hours I would feel the heartbreak, "You don't want to be with me," I said.

"It isn't that at all," she said quickly. I cocked my head, hoping that doing that would also relieve the pressure in my eyes. I asked myself if I would cry before putting up a good many no crying signs just next to the eye socket exits of my brain.

In the chasm between rooms and door and stairs with me, she said, "I thought they would run their hands along me a certain way, with a certain taste," she sucked on her cheek and clarified, "in a certain way. Maybe it was me or maybe it was them. One of us wasn't working for me, though, and I found it easier to rid myself of them than of myself." She smiled a bit at the end of the sentence and I realized she had had an epiphany while speaking.

I hurriedly replied with, "I don't want you to feel like you ever need to get rid of either of us." She pushed her eyes around the baseboards and bottom corners of the walls, not looking at me. I continued, "I don't have any maps, any direction, anything." I let my arms rise and fall, "But I want to explore you, not just your body, but your mind, and mouth." I cringed- my words were not forming the way I intended, "I want to get lost with you, but I don't want you to lose yourself. Or lose interest in me." I could only hope they fell on ears that understood.

A flicker of a smile lightened her redwood-colored eyes, "When most people get lost, they spin around in a circle looking for a reference point, then they explode off."

"I won't do that," I promised.

"People can't make that promise."

"How do you know that?" I asked.

Her smile faded, then re-emerged, "It's my job to know what people do when they're afraid."

"I am afraid," I said.

"I want to help," she said and it reminded me of our first time together, only days ago.

"I don't want to hurt," I promised.

"Loving steadfastly and with strength is not an instilled strength but one that takes challenges and effort. That recognizes tribulations and the power of forgiveness." She leveled her eyes with mine, "It isn't an object that can be thrown away when it doesn't make you happy or doesn't work for a few small moments but a relationship and a measure of two people's character to be lived steadfastly and with strength," she said with a simple tone.

"Got it," I said to her.

"I don't want to start caring about the way my makeup looks or where to eat or any of the normal things other people make you care about."

"Keep the dark circles under your eyes. Let the world know you're tired of it." I said, "Eat with or without me, don't ever wait for me. I'll be here for you but you be here for you, too." I looked into the deep recesses of her eyes. A light inside them was flickering on and off and I tried to steal glimpses of what was there.

"When you build walls to others, you have to climb over them, too." She let her head tilt and took a step toward me. Her hair hit my face and her hips hit mine. My arms had been frozen, nervous, and immobile until I lifted them and held her shoulder-blades in my hands, willing her to try to steady her heartbeat by being pressed close to mine.

That night, after I had salvaged items from the street and the furniture from my apartment, I held Cecilia again.

I spoke below a whisper as she breathed in dreams, "I am not a whole person. I may never be as whole as I need to be happy. If I could do one thing half as well as you, I'd be perfectly happy." She shifted and rolled as my heart did the same. Was it love or fear of loss that was guiding it, I asked myself. Guided by only intuition, like a boat in a storm hoping for land.

The only things that would happen would happen while out to sea, but I desperately wanted to be standing solidly on land.

She rolled over and an arm leapt at me as her mouth moved, like fast twitches instead of the normal read of a mouth I can get.

In her muddled speech she asked me, "Do you remember being on clouds with me?" She shifted her head and said, "Pu--- you left, why?"

I shook my head as I remembered she had told me to go to a higher spirit plane, and I did and left her, but I faltered when I felt a lumpy mass in my throat.

I didn't get a chance to speak because she said,"Why? Leave? Not that," and batted a hand against my face before her breathing regulated and was back to sleep.

Chapter Eleven

I hoped to get just as many nights with her as the number of breaths I took. I sometimes began to fear that she did not wish the same. There was something about the way she would tell me, bravely, that she was more inclined to spend a day alone. Over the course of the day, her frown would lighten buoyantly as she did things like draw teeth in sharpie along the trim of the wall. She would tell me that the mirror had cheered her up. She had a way of getting only her own jokes. She was different around other people, but I soon grew to see a painted smile. I kissed her scars because I knew she could kiss mine. I asked myself if relationships are only a way to fix what childhood may have broken.

Before she would get up in the mornings, about a week after we got furniture in there, I would hurry out of bed, nauseous at her perfect form strangled or suffocated in the sheets to look out the window or pace the house. For a while I would stare out the window of the bedroom. The slate grey of early dawn receded into the west and the sun's candle melted on the small segment of skyline in the east as it raised itself up. I could tell the winter was coming in the cold of the mornings.

The Oakland skyline from the very west was dynamic, bouncing up and down in industrial rectangles. It was a very amazing place, one where culture had been created and destroyed and created again, only to be destroyed. Boxy houses once owned by primarily people of color were now a desolate sight. They had been forced out of their homes for white families to move in after they had made the community a wonderful place to be.

Even now, I would notice white realtors rolling through, making notes and asking my white friends questions when I wasn't around about the neighborhood and trying to estimate the value of displacing people again for their profit. A huge post-office had once leveled communities on top of communities of homes. Now it stood in all its glory, covering miles of area where people of color had once lived and thrived. All of the generations of displaced youth were grown up now and heard from the older folks that had stuck around the sad past. They heard and talked about it, because there is always power in spoken history, even when another culture has tried to strip you of it.

Being allies and not adversaries with others was more important than hating the past, but I still resented the individuals that treated me and the people around me poorly. I couldn't help it. Together, though, we could understand the past and not neglect it. Together we could make the way we are connected something to be proud of.

Systems like white oppression that breed people into being aware of stigmas and not of their privilege was being worked every single day, in every single way conceivable. Why people like to define others is beyond me. But I saw it happen. I saw people with Eurocentric values tell Tre, who was from Atlanta, that his accent was "weird" and that upset me. I was told that I wasn't "like other black people" because I "spoke so well," which upset me further.

The people saying those things are not aware that they are trying to not only define us by standards that their culture values, they are also unwittingly trying to redefine what they do not understand so that we fit into their culture more easily. If the future did not hold appropriate and equal rights for all, I didn't know what I would do.

A train whipped from the sunrise and ducked into the tube going to the city. I scoffed and the fog that hit the window pane from my mouth turned the view into soft shapes of purple and pink. I touched the tiny water, trying to think of nothing.

Turns out trying to think of nothing was a lot harder thank thinking of what hadn't been done yet. Things that should have been done. Reminders of those things were everywhere. White crosses were raised on the lawn of the church on San Pablo Boulevard for every young person killed in a homicide in Oakland. The January 1st memorial for Oscar Grant's death was in Fruitvale. The corner where Huey Newton's death took place.

They were all reminders that we all needed to change the way we behave. It wasn't people like her dad that needed to change. The movement against white oppression reminded me of the lengths women had come by saying things like, "Girls don't need to be told not get raped; boys need to be told to not rape." Those lengths represented the same agenda.

I thought of women and looked at the bed as the light had fallen on Cecilia and was in the middle of an embrace of her muscles. I didn't need to think she was strong. She was strong, whether or not a man like me was going to tell her or not. A picture close to the door rattled and I looked back to her.

The sunrise added light to her bunched-up hair to make the curls look like steaming coals. I shuddered to think of anyone walking over them in another coal walk. I shuddered thinking of the bitter tasting Brugmansia tea. When I had the rest of what Leonard had left to be in my hands, I had rid of this earth, not knowing what I was doing, at all. Some things are above the law of man, I thought, Or below it. I tapped the wood paneling of the window, trying to remember who had said that.

There was some idea about what Leonard deserved that I must not have understood. I had executed my own personal justice on him, already, and no amount of thinking would reverse it. And yet, I was attracted to it like a bee to sugar. I should have been taking pollen from flowers, but the artificial sugar called to me in a different, addictive way. I wanted to wrap my mind around what it was I had really done to him and take that knowledge away from wherever it was, but it was distant and far from me.

Was that what justice should descend into when your world was ruled by crooks? Leonard was small compared to the big kleptocracies that ruled all of the country, but still bigger than the small kind that were scuffling to take Leonard Kiljun's place. The small guys robbing and beating and maybe murdering were still the small guys in comparison. Is that why I had been asked by Gods to leave them alone? Let them claw over one another until they couldn't pick up their feet without somebody else pulling their leg back down, was that what I was supposed to do?

I spent an hour reading entry scripts on coding forums before Cecilia woke. Next to my laptop was a filled flower vase. She brushed the petals away like she was sweeping stray hairs from a face before a smile tucked into her cheeks that caught my eye. Like a cliff, her cheekbones held her abundant apple-colored cheeks above them and I kissed each before licking a thumb and wiping away the salty accumulations on the edges of her eyes. She scowled and walked toward the bedroom door.

I glanced at the entry codes one last time, longing to have my body extrapolate my mind from it and be able to go inside the internet. It wasn't very mindful or meditative to envision yourself removing your mind from your body, so I shut the laptop and pushed back my chair to walk with her.

"I want to try volunteering," I told her.

As her feet hit the stair-boards she chuckled, "Sounds like something coming from a privileged kid," and rounded the corner into the living room.

I paused there to think before padding into the kitchen and speaking. "I have been led to believe people in the neighborhood wanted more community involvement," I said it with an air of self-chastisement I didn't necessarily deserve, but felt entitled to since she had put the idea in my head.

"You don't know what they need. Most of them want food and warmth but really need a lifetime of happiness that is free of pain." She handed me a can of beans to open then said, "Not one person under the level of the super rich is going to get that. At least, not in this country." She glanced out the window, "Or in this part of it."

"You need the dark to see the light," I tried. I set a pan on a burner to warm.

She said, "Have you looked outside, this lower bottoms -as it says on the map- community," she put an emphasis on the latter word, "is dark 364 days a year." She stirred together blue corn powder and water, then ladled it onto a pan with sizzling oil, "But, sure, volunteer, only after you've made sure your good intentions are educated."

"Like what?" I mashed the beans against the side of the pan.

"Remind people of that one bright, shiny, good day. Every day. Then the clouds might part." She flipped one of the tortilla pancakes. She had a press to make tortillas but when we were both groggy and waking up we didn't use it too much then.

"Thanks, I'll keep it all in mind," I said.

"Yeah in your subconscious," she said. I was taking out two plates when there was a knock at the door. We exchanged looks and I took out a third. The sounds were sharp as I placed them on the table and walked to the front door.

"Hey Tre." I said as I opened the door.

"Hey man," he said, "do you mind?" I shook my head, no. He ducked in and we walked back to the kitchen together.

"Tre's here," I said.

"Figured as much," Cecilia mused as she prodded the third purple circle to be panned on.

Tre sat down heavily at the corner table, "Thanks guys."

We both nodded before exchanging heavier looks than we had when he first arrived, "You seem more down than usual," I said.

He looked down and said, "Do I?"

"What's going on?" I asked more directly.

"My grandma's no good right now," he sighed as Cecilia put a plate beneath him. I could smell the verde salsa as it heated up atop the beans and purple corn tortilla.

"I'm sorry to hear that." Cecilia said, "How is your family taking it?"

Tre shrugged heavily and picked up a fork intentionless, "My aunt is going back to Atlanta to live with her." I inhaled quickly- he lived underneath her house in a hobbit hole-like studio.

He said quickly, "But the really messed up part is my mom calls me and tells me she would be better of if her mom died. How messed up is that, man?" Cecilia turned away from us and plated more food.

"I know I couldn't handle that," I said as I grabbed my plate.

"Especially for me. How should I feel about her after I hear that, I was working at an early age, man, to feed my little sisters and pay her bills, man, and she says something like that. I don't ever want to think things like that, that I'd be better off if my momma was just gone- but it's in my genes! I probably will feel that way later if she is now!" He looked about to cry but tore into the food instead. Cecilia sat and ate slowly and I took a bite before thinking about what my dad had told me.

"Each child should try to be better than the generation that raised them," I said before eating again.

"No place to live so how do I do that?" He mused darkly.

I looked at Cecilia before I spoke, "Live here," I suggested.

"Nah you guys got your own thing going," he said.

Cecilia held his hand against the unfinished wood of the table, "It would be no problem."

He tilted his head, "That would be nice." He then said, "You know what? Thank you."

We nodded together, touching knees and feeling happier than ever. After breakfast, Cecilia took a shower and I put her towels in the drier that I had installed earlier that week. Tre hopped the back fence to cross the lot and get coffee. When I heard the squeak of the faucet turn off -which was still operated by turning a wrench- I took the stairs in twos to get to her.

She shrieked just as I got to the middle landing and at the top, she was asking aloud, "Where are they? I need a towel!"

"Right here," I said as I held the first one out to wrap around her.

She looked at me, excited, and said, "They're so warm!"

I side-grinned as she took the other and wrapped it around her hair and said, "For you, anything."

She touched her cheek to her shoulder and I kissed her neck as water slid down it. She touched my chin, looking into my eyes, then retreated back into the bathroom. I swayed in the hallway for a moment before slipping into the back bedroom that Tre could live in. Light from the windows settled on the one pile of debris in the room: plywood and screws, dusty with disuse. It overlooked the lot, boat, cafe, and our backyard and was shadowed by the rails that the transit took just before being funneled into the tunnel. I saw Tre trudging back though the weeds in the lot. It wouldn't take a lot of work to get his room in order. The real work would be in the weed-eaten lot where he had been.

"I'm going to go out," I spoke into the bathroom and grabbed my coat and debit card.

"Hey," I said at the door.

"Here," Tre handed me two cups and picked his up off of the stoop.

"How'd you manage to carry all these?" I asked, recollecting the image of him walking across the lot with them.

He waved his hand in the air, "Magic."

"Want to go to the hardware store?" I asked him.

"Sounds like a good distraction" He said with a smile as he adjusted his hat over his locked hair. I grabbed my car keys out of my pocket and threw them to him before running up the stairs to hand Cecilia her drink. She had turned around and was looking out of the bathroom at me.

"Where?-" She began to ask before I pecked a kiss on her lips.

"Don't worry about it," I said.

Outside, the walnuts were pelting anything in their fall's path as the early winter winds shook them. Their hulls covered the stoop, front yard, and beyond the fence to the side-walk. Tre was standing next to my car, which had sustained some new scratches and dents from the walnuts.

"Hand me those," I said as I grabbed the keys from him, "I thought you would unlock it and get in."

He shrugged as he did get in and asked, "Got music?"

I put it on an Atmosphere, Immortal Technique, Asap Rock, and Sage Francis playlist. There wasn't much talking to be done over their spitted words as I took us toward the hardware store.

When we got out, he said, "Your music tastes are mostly white, man."

I asked, "Does it matter? They're all spitting about things I relate to, especially living here, so I get down."

"Fair enough," I said. "Who do you recommend?"

He smiled, "Biggie! Pac! The RZA and GZA and the warriors of the clan!"

I laughed, "Have you read their book?"

"The Wu-Tang's? Yeah, parts of it. That's how I learned how to play chess."

"They're legitimate geniuses," I said.

When we were inside, he asked, "What are we getting here?"

"Garden supplies," I said.

"Genius," he said. I couldn't gauge by his tone if he was joking or not.

I grabbed hand tools, long shovels, and hoes as well as a variety of poop and soil. Tre knew some winter vegetables and greens and picked out some gloves and sun-hats when he realized I wasn't on any budgets.

He finally asked after it was all loaded in my car, "What are you planning?"

"I'll have to graph something," I said before cut me off.

"Graphing is where I draw the line." He looked at me with a grin that made me stop and think.

"That's funny," I said, "I haven't heard you cracking jokes like you used to today."

He asked, "What mp3 hookups do you have in here?" I showed him my cord and he plugged it into his phone and

"Did you go see your folks?" He asked me and I nodded, "Thought so, you could have said something. You got bad news down there, didn't you?"

"You've been dealing with your own stuff." I told him, though it felt like putting up a mirror was a facade, so I said, "But I did," he looked across at me in my car with sympathy, "and I did some stuff I didn't want to and maybe Cecilia thinks of me differently because of it." I felt myself convulsing with words and I held the steering wheel like it was my gurney, "Both my mother and my dad don't even want me, too." My tears mixed with spit as they fell into my mouth. I moved my head and they made a stream on the black plastic above the airbag.

Tre patted my back, "We're not going to jump off a cliff and swim away, though, live through this." He kept patting my back and said, "You are the smartest guy I know. You got this."

I sniffed up the loose phlegm and he told me, "Say to yourself, 'I got this.'"

I sniffed again and moused out, "Got this?"

"You got this!" He yelled.

"You got this," I said looking at him belligerently.

"Close enough." He laughed, "Now get a step on it, I don't like the look of this guy."

I followed his gaze and was looking at the pink face of Carlyle Bruisyn and some of his friends, whose faces I recognized from my dad's desk, across the street. I cursed and ducked, which could have only alerted them. Tre moved toward me and turned the keys in the ignition. I looked behind my shoulder and then forward before slipping the clutch and getting us away.

Tre didn't question the incident and plugged his phone in after a few moments and started the rap radio again. We didn't speak about the scare, but he did speak up when we were on San Pablo Street.

"I lost my job, man."

"Weren't you freelancing?"

"No, a company hired me and kept me on for a long-term contract, but broke it when they got a new CEO."

"That's the worst kind of luck," I said, steering and keeping my thoughts on the road. When I gave it thought, though, I realized there was something we could do. "Do you have a website?" I asked him.

"Yep, why?" he asked back.

"I want you to give me the URL of yours and the company website you were working for when we get back to the house," I told him.

He spoke up again when I stopped back in West Oakland. I surveyed a fig tree, parked next to the street, and jumped on the edges of the hood of my car to get as many as I could.

"What are you doing now?" he asked up to me.

I handed him three as I got back in, "Good, huh?"

"So this is why they're in the bible," he said as he at the seedy red and purple insides of the fruit. "They're good. So good."

"So after the graphs, which I still draw the line at, what do you see?" he asked when I was driving again.

"Work, want to start it with me today?" I asked.

"Of course," he said. "What do you think you're doing with Cecilia?"

His question put me off at first, but I had to remember he had watched us for months when we were just two friends, three friends really, getting to know each other.

He continued while I thought, "I know how you feel about him," I side-eyed him with a question on my lips before he spoke again, "but Bob Marley said, 'There is no greater coward than the man that awakens a woman's love with no intention of loving her.'"

I looked at him plainly before parking in front of the house before speaking, "I had tried to make generalizations about all people after feeling more abandoned than protected a few years ago." He sighed and I said as we got out, "I recognized that people shared similar good qualities than bad ones. Cecilia has more good qualities than any other person I know."

"Good. Be good," he said as he walked up to the gate.

As I stepped onto the sidewalk I saw my actions anew. I put into question my every action. I could no longer step off the street without analyzing my every motion towards that goal. I had made my every action represent myself in everything I did to avoid the anxieties I put myself through. With the tools I was given was I now supposed to analyze every one of my actions? I fell into the thoughts, as I always did, even if knew much more than I should but I had so much less to lose than I should, too. I could no longer feel half of myself.

The sun hit my eyes and I jumped back from the sidewalk. Tre looked back at me.

"Tools," I said, pointing to the trunk. I was distracting myself from my own thoughts, but which was more productive, the distraction or the thoughts, I knew not.

He jumped a few paces back to the car door and we both unloaded them next to the chain-link fence to the left of the house. We passed under the fence and, in two trips, had moved the gardening supplies to one side of the reclaimed boat in the weedy lot.

I hacked a rectangle out of the crab-grass and weeds with the hand-hoe after I had handed a big one to Tre. A garden had already been started and managed on the side of the boat closest to the cafe. Sol had shown it to me, pulling out a squash and telling me what was there I was free to use when she did. We decided we would make beds in the same way the other garden had set up, in neat rows, and didn't plan any plants they had already made happen there.

Tre and I cleared that first rectangle, cleared a path around it, dug out a few feet of sandy soil, then filled it back up with poopy fertilizer and soil. We also started a few feet of the next one on that first day of work. With some hammers and nails from the back porch of the house and some scrap-wood we made a hutch for the gardening supplies.

Back inside, I asked Tre for the information about his work and he dictated to me while I typed.

"What are you doing now?" he asked.

"Going into the matrix," I told him, laughing, as I swerved between windows and searched a few lines of code I hadn't ever used. "Now," I told him, finishing up, "their website redirects back to yours. So when this new big CEO calls you, begging for you to change it back, tell him he can give you your job back. And then tell me and I'll actually change it."

"Man," Tre put a hand on my shoulder, "I don't know what to say except thank you."

"I accept thank you's," I told him.

Tre walked home for lunch and to tell his aunt that he would be moving out before her and I said so long to him for the day. Cecilia looked delighted at the figs and made a pan tarte tatin with them while I shredded a squash and lightly fried the stringy pieces with pine nuts and sesame oil.

I said to Cecilia as we cooked, "It was a hard way to learn about it, but after the experience with you and your mom and Leonard, I feel closer to understanding death."

She shook her head, "I can't straddle the idea of dying. As a child, I wanted to kill myself," she said while checking the tarte with a toothpick. "I'm no closer to understanding. I never will until I actually die. I would look up and say, 'Mama, I want to die just to know what it feels like.' I was so young!"

I looked at her tenderly, "But you are one of the things I want to protect and to let live as freely as you can."

She shrugged and said, "First of all, not necessary. I got a handle on my own life, thank you. But, I didn't know what would happen if I died or if my mom died. Or if my cat died, even. That's hard to not know. It's something I don't think I know even after our spiritual experience with my mom. As much as I try, there is only one point in which I know what death entails. What if I don't even know. What if I pass from this body to another instantly? Will I never get to know? Will it just be darkness or whiteness? With death comes the meaning of my life," she paused, the finished with, "And not even that is a given." She looked at what I had cooked, squinted her eyes to her nose and began doling some tortilla batter she had saved onto the still-hot pan I had used for the squash.

"I didn't mean for you to make more," I said. "It's no problem. There are rice and beans on the table." I placed the squiggly greens on the table next to the steaming containers.

As she sat down, Cecilia sighed. I held her hand with both of mine and she leaned her head over until it was laying on the table, too.

I spoke, "I know what bad moods are like. What it's like to have it on your shoulders, go ahead."

She sighed and talked toward me, "I wonder if I've gone too far, planned ahead too much and fallen in love with my made-up future. What happens when plans change and I'm forced to cope with plans that I hadn't imagined? I begin to think these plans aren't what I want, though. I could be deluded and I wouldn't really know it."

"That last part got me." I asked, "How much trust can you have in your future if you're still thinking of the past?"

"Exactly, how much trust can anybody really have?" She started eating and said, "I am no exception."

I thought about how many breakdowns I had been having lately. Points where I felt like I couldn't breathe and could only cry, which wasn't the person I thought I would become. I did not know I was letting my self-concept get out of hand; I really thought I was everything I wanted to be.

I looked at Cecilia and reminded myself that we were all trying our best and that nobody had anything to prove, really. I didn't have to prove anything. Everyone is out to prove something, but no one has anything to prove or is better than anybody else.

I said after chewing my stringy squash, "I think my main fear is growing out of this stage of knowing."

She nodded, "Your brain stops functioning in a lot of ways and grows out of this stage of its life where it just questions everything."

I said, "Maybe you get broken by the world, looking around and seeing what has happened, where the breaks are, and what can be done to fix it all."

She asked, "But do you realize there is no point in questioning it. That there are no good effects to working against the system, morals are useful but used less, and that you have learned everything you need to learn."

I shrugged off her rhetorical question, "Growing up means that you lose a certain lust. A non-toxic lust. A regenerative lust for knowledge and growth. I do not want to loose that."

"I attribute it to perception." She finished her food and picked up both of our plates, "Take, for instance, the plight of one person to the next's. Each person is in a both awesome and awful situation, but each handles their environment based on experience. Past outcomes."

"Again with the past," I said, "it makes me stumble." I had begun thinking of my dad when she said that your brain stops functioning without even knowing it. What was it that had caused his mind to fail, and was it avoidable? I pressed a hand to my heavy heart and wondered if I would try to reach out to him and call. Only I could know, but I didn't, really.

She said as we stood up, "Are we cleaning the third bedroom today?" I nodded and she continued as we got dustpans and trash cans, "Oftentimes I will find I have a new perspective. It is a sudden thing and before, when the feeling was a new one to me, I searched for a way to deal with it and contain it somehow. When I did nothing it was the best possible outcome. I didn't do anything, I merely experienced this world in a different way."

I cocked my head, thinking as we went upstairs. The room's three windows let in no light as the walnut tree obstructed all light and any view. The floor had been torn out and re-installed recently, but some random debris and dust remained.

Cecilia spoke as we picked up trash and stacked it into a contractor's bag, "Many experiences like that have given me great insights. The feeling was once quite unnatural, but now that I have experienced so many things, it is very normal and always pleasing, in a way."

"Once a skill or talent has been questioned and analyzed and examined, it is always enjoyable for me," I said as I picked up a broom. We swept the top room clean and fell into one another's dusty, greasy arms for a siesta.

Chapter Twelve

In the mornings I awoke in order to work and make the ground grow with the garden. It was a way of keeping peace with my future. I would be more present when I worked.

My hands would toil in the sun-drenched black and browns of dirt. My back and legs grew accustomed to squatting to lift, push, or pull. I found the right way to cup my hands, fold my shoulders, and move for every specific task I set to do. Muscle memory developed after so many months.

There were social aspects of the project that Sol volunteered me for. Recruiting, doing introductions for volunteers, then being able to oversee them was my way of seeing new insights and perspectives. Not many knew who operated the garden project. I instructed subjectively, letting everybody know how I had come to whatever conclusion through learning from them. Those that had first started their garden asked for help building a chicken coop and maintaining them. I built chicken runs where new beds were going to grow to have them scratch the ground until it was viable. The lot blossomed and the hard-work putting in plants during the winter meant a bountiful garden by spring. The figs and walnuts were no longer in season, but there were enough other things planted by us to sell to co-ops, at markets, and local groceries. Nonetheless, my eyes caught on the leathery, oblong leaves of the fig tree and awakened an odd desire that I couldn't quite quell.

The days I had found myself grieving about what had become of Leonard and my cousins, I also happened to be working sunrise to sundown. When I came home from working the soil, I washed my hands and booted up the pc to continue my daily revolt against every system I could enter and disrupt.

One day Cecilia came to the house after being at her mother's. She handed me a glass bottle of jasmine water and one of the bell-shaped yellow flowers from the garden. I set both of them down on a side-table and cocked my head in question.

"She's in love with Leonard and Austin, now." She groaned as she fell into the table with her face, "My mother's moving to live with them. Whatever that means."

"They live on the spirit plane! Does that mean she's going to die?" I asked.

She groaned again and slammed her balled-up fists on the table. Her hair and fists were all I could see of her as she stayed there, sad and lonely.

"Well, what did she tell you?" I became preoccupied with starting the gas on the stove. It clicked and with a *fahoom* it began blazing blue-hot flames.

"I'm inviting Shellie over," she said before standing up and pushed off of her chair and past the doorframe, "I need to not think."

I was still mastering the many variations of the vegetable quiche when Shellie and Cecilia sat at the itches table across from one another. I would be convinced on appearances alone that Shellie was not a human, but she spoke of such human interest issues that I'm still not sure.

"Do you love cooking more than anything?" She asked me in the kitchen.

I said, "Not as much as I garden," thinking she would tell me about some good gardening supply store or cooking tips.

Instead, she said, "When you give flowers to someone who doesn't know how to grow them, they say, 'Thanks.' But when you give them to someone who does garden they say, 'Wow! You went through all of this trouble! How long did it take them? Did you use a fertilizer? What ratios did you use? Can you show me that?' It is the same way with love." I gave her my full attention as she spoke, now, "If you're giving it to someone who doesn't love they won't really know what to do with the love you give them." Cecilia started applauding her, grinning as her point became more clear.

"You're right," I said as I left the kitchen, wondering what she was alluding to about me.

When I came in to check on a non-quickie quiche that was taking extra-long in the oven I heard her say, "There's no easier way to get rid of a girl than to kindly become upset by some part of her body," I walked away but still heard her talking, "the vagina, boobs, or other often-sexualized body part is especially good for this. She'll think about what you said, how you meant it, how she should have reacted, and will mull over the truthfulness of the statement for perhaps months to come. Eventually finding some kind of closure and trying to forget the incident entirely. Usually the person to make the comment has long been forced out of the woman's life by this time."

Cecilia reacted quickly, "Respective to the woman in question."

She got side-tracked, "I do like your features, Cecilia. I do believe facial expressions are determinative over the facial features themselves."

Cecilia thanked her and I came into the kitchen."I don't even know where to begin with college," Cecilia said to us both.

Shellie nodded and spoke heavily, "Do not passively absorb, but instead, follow the cross references of the most personally interesting subjects," she advised.

I tried to specify, "Follow your interests."

Cecilia laughed and said, "Both education and capitol discrimination have become more important than doing anything useful in this place."

"Man is covered in a soft exterior and a complex interior. What we do with ourselves is the mystery of life," I added.

"I love when someone thinks I'm turned on because of a little wet spot," out of nowhere, Shellie began to speak over me to Cecilia, "I want to tell them that that little discharge is just my body's way of cleansing old cells or bacteria to keep out infection and is its own little way of maintaining optimal health, but it's hard to say, you know?"

I left through the backdoor with my sunhat and gardening gloves to work on a bed of transplanted chard. The red and yellow stalks smelled like candy when I pruned them and I didn't wash my hands before crawling into bed with Cecilia that night.

I looked at her asleep and thought, I want to understand you the way you understand me. I want to enjoy what you enjoy and suffer with you. The sad truth is that we will loose each other sooner or later and I've just come to terms with my love for you. You and I are alike. We can't become close without sharing compassion. I am loyal to you because you are loyal to logic. While I seek, you find and hide what I truly want and need.

I saw her curled up then, the way she would curl up when we argued to think out a response and thought, Only after finishing fidgeting will you tell me in verses I don't expect to understand what it is inside your head, Cecilia. I'll let my subconscious work it out, like I always seem to do.

As I watched her, I remembered the last time I had told her what she was to me, she had said, "Why can't I see in myself what you see in me? I only see the burdens I carry."

"Why haven't these things come up between us before?" I had asked her.

She had said, "We have a bitter, restrained, wonderful thing going right now." I still didn't know what to think of that.

I knew then that there were thoughts like scoundrels inside of her, but each time I saw her like this, curled up with all of her sadness and glory, I fell with her and was the happy victim

I went to see Edna the next day. Her decision to leave was heavy in my kind, weighing down the buoyancy Cecilia brought to my life.

"So you have heard," she said at the gate. She was burying and burning her hair again, like the first time I had met her.

"Today, while thinking about love, I began to cry," she became candid quickly. "Not now, I thought as I pressed my palms into my eyes, not while it is light out. Only in dreams can I do this. You see: I can only see the loves of my life when I am dreaming or in the spirit world."

I shook my hair as she sat down on one of the steps. I sat next to her and sighed out, "I know I'll miss you. Cecilia, will especially, Edna." She waved her hand and I stopped talking.

"My going away will put into perspective the vast love she does feel for you. You are worth this," she said peacefully watching the sky. Mornings were getting warmer.

I said, "I want to do something for her. Make her happy in an attempt to rectify the things she knows and will not stop worrying about."

She told me, "She would like to be held by you. Every you, she want to hold all of those parts of you that she loves. She doesn't want to remember some of you when you aren't around, like now, but all of you."

"I don't just want her to be surprised by some of me, I think most of all I want her to be comfortable with most of me, or all of me," I enthusiastically said to her.

She nodded gracefully to the morning sun, "The parts of her that genuinely care and want to reach out to hold you, will."

I said goodbye to her awkwardly, with a hug and peck on the cheek before pushing my hands in my pockets and walking to the cafe. My shoes clapped on the street and when I passed the trash can that had Fresh Prince scrawled across it, I thought of Jeff and how I had lost him and the rest of the monks after putting Leonard in the sky.

The barista shook her black bangs at me snottily and I thought of reaching out to someone I didn't know too well. I tried talking to her, but her words made the dark coffee shake to my hand. I set it down and dabbed at the tender burn with a few brown napkins. I picked up my coffee and went all the way to the back of the porch.

I peeked into the radio station through the window and noticed Chloe was there. She looked over at me and smiled before getting up and opening the door.

"What's on your mind?" She asked, then said, "I'm between sets."

I replied, "If A then C. If no C no A."

"What?" She asked as she sat down and lit one of her cigarettes.

"I told you," she offered me a cigarette and I said, "what's on my mind. If two things exist with one another, then one is removed, what happens?"

She nodded, smiling behind her dark lipstick, "I get you."

"What happens when people leave?" I asked her.

"What will happen when you leave her?" I looked at her skeptically and she said, "What? I know things, too."

I shrugged and told her, "I could not live without her once we were together for one another."

"Maybe it was-" she stopped talking as the barista walked onto the patio, picking up unused plates and barely glancing at us, then continued, "A romance that was based on the time of your life it started in. Remember people wean off of relationships differently.

Not everybody stops cold-turkey and not everyone stops seeing one another gradually. No two relationships are the same."

"Well, I'm not planning on breaking things off." I informed her, "It is other people that are going away."

"Want to say something on air?" She asked.

"Baroque musicians loved extravagance and intense dramas and played with operas taken from Greek Myth. They filled their art program with complex, emotional, psychological, and inventive aspects and would have been nothing without the Council of Trent's Catholic reformation and support," I said.

She laughed and stamped out her cigarette, "I'll take that as a 'No,' then."

"Probably shouldn't," I told her.

She nodded and said, "She's a cute girl, too," before going back into the radio station. I looked around the patio, the cold of winter made people less likely to come out. Scuba Steve lounged in a chair by the door and looked up and threw me a peace-sign as I walked past.

I got a coffee for Cecilia and walked through the back, past gardens and the boat, to the house.

Shellie was over again, saying, "I'm saying to them that being down with the predatory behavior of guys somehow makes you a girl that can hang while really you're pushing the oppressors up. They ask, 'How does it feel to be called a feminist?' Well, how does it feel to have a penis? It's the opposite of that."

I went back on the computer and tracked some of Carlyle Bruisyn's latest activity before hacking into some major companies and setting program pots. There was a cache of different codes that would be randomly applied once an admin from the company opened the html source code, hindering them from seeing at anybody's files but their own. Because their website would crash for a day, they would be more susceptible to someone finding their way even farther into their system, which I planned to do. After doing that to them, I poked around bigger companies'n sites. By the end of the day, stocks in several of the largest companies had radically declined and two were temporarily closing their main offices. I saved all of my original files and planned to do it again, soon.

I went inside the kitchen to hear Cecilia quoting Dostoyevsky to Shellie, "'There is nothing easier than lopping off heads and nothing harder than developing ideas.'"

"Well said," she said.

"Do you know why you jerk awake at night?"Cecilia asked when we were alone.

I guessed, "You're remembering the futility of it all?"

She laughed and said, "It's because your heart decreased so rapidly while you were sleeping that your body jerks you to make sure you're still alive."

"So I'm almost dying."

"I couldn't take it if you died." She told me, looking into my eyes while the setting sun brought out flecks of amber in hers. I held her shoulders, looking at her eyes candidly, before holding her in my hug.

"I already miss you so much," she said.

"But I'm right here," I spoke into her hair. "Let's go re-program some road signs," I tried.

She looked up at me with a smile on her lips and we spent the night driving until we found one, programmed it to a crude saying for motorists to enjoy, then went to curry around 2 am. We didn't get back to West Oakland until the BART had long since stopped running and instead had begun doing test runs just before the sun rose.

Having Tre there meant we planned and worked on the garden more and were becoming devoted to it. I worked with groups outside of the direct neighborhood and in Northern and Central Oakland instead of just the Lower Bottoms. Sol and I invited children and families to help and the community became absorbed in its own health for small spurts, but there were aspects missing about the project that made them leave, eventually.

When I washed off the dirt, I was surprised by how pleased it made me to watch the brown slip off of my skin. At some point in almost every black child's life, they have truly wished the color in their skin would slip off and they'd be a white child. The illusion made me grip the sides of the sink and double over in tears, because I knew that the feelings I had had were not specific to me. I had been told every day of my life that I would be better if I were white, in some way or another, and the knowledge that that vicious cycle did not start and stop with me made me ache to run out and skip rope, play, teach all of the young black children I could find. I feared something about associating with me, a young man that didn't have to work for his money, put them off. I worried that that put the entire community off of me.

Chapter Thirteen

The winter came down on us all like a strangling blanket. Frost would lick the green grass in front of the house up overnight. In the morning, when the sun would first hit the frost-covered tops of every house, steam would billow off of them, making a rare sighting of a working fireplace just an illusion. I was under the delusion that the lack of central-heating wouldn't impact us in some small way.

The house was a sad place, looking back at that time, but there were a lot of reasons for that. The winters were colder in Oakland than in San Francisco and few had internal heating, like us. Every cold day felt like a battle against death. We would stay inside more, holed up and bored by everything that wasn't warming.

I noticed talks with Cecilia weaning themselves out of our relationship. We talked while sanding the walls about painting them, talked over painting them about baseboards, and talked about the next project while putting in the baseboards. I worked to forget my yearning for the lyrical lips we had once used. Nothing meaningful exists outside of discourse, I reminded myself while struggling with new and exciting words for her. I wanted to ask her, "Can we talk tomorrow? Or, better yet, today, tonight even?" but bit my tongue, re-phrased in my head, "I do miss knowing that you exist and it is nice to think you want to make sure I'm not turning dumb or dull." Both seemed heavily laced with pleading undertones and my tongue withdrew.

I worked in the garden, found new places to volunteer, drank endless coffee at Introvert cafe, and avoided what I couldn't do for us. I felt troubled, a knowledge that I was doing something wrong but no idea what. I diverted the thoughts I had for my relationship to picking up projects in the community. It was true, resources and their accessibility for the residents of that neighborhood were scarce.

The resources I saw in Oakland were: fruit dropping off the trees in the street; gardens like mine all over the place; great food bank distribution program; the co-op; and the WIC program, set up to benefit growing children's bodies and their mothers. Much like a food-stamp program, it only worked at one liquor store on the boundary of two projects and offered, among other poor choices, $7.00 frozen vegetables, 14-month old apples, and three dollar hot dogs. That particular program's strength in the community was obviously not a resource that needed to could be utilized as well as the others. The co-op on 7th street specialized in high-grade meat, wonderful local produce, and a decent bulk section. It was easily the gem to be polished, honed, and not outsourced. Chloe from the radio station had once applied there and she got the impression that they were really trying to serve the under-privileged and not people with a wealth of opportunities already in front of them, which she inevitably came to understand as better for the neighborhood. The co-op met the fiscal strength of the surrounding economy with the right resources.

There are a total number of resources and a relative that you need to look at comparatively. The resource here that was relative to the community after being looked at comparatively with what people here needed: food, better heating, income opportunities. But first, food was good. Most people all across the country needed better heating right now.

In the garden I heard Tre ask me while we were aerating the ground, "What do you think of brothers getting shot lately?" I thought suddenly of Carlyle Bruisyn and the other unknown three gangsters trying to take Leonard place. I shook off the imagery of Leonard being the headless chicken running blood on a blue river canvas.

Because I had remained silent, he said, "I know it scares white people from moving in."

"I think most people that are white," I stated, "really don't know we can all be brothers."

He laughed then spoke, "I know of a few brothers that know we can't. You're not like all black people, Ryan."

I told him, "You know that that's a lot like me saying the same to you."

"Which is just as rude, saying, 'You're not like all black people,' is so rude! And there I go, saying it." I nodded sternly and he said, "Brothers have learned to avoid white men as a safety precaution," he said, "nothing else."

"Well, what kind of cycles do you see in the system that," I worked for words, "don't let us collaborate as humans well?"

217

"Prejudices, disrespect of centuries," he began, "you?"

I burrowed my shovel into the ground and leaned on it to think, then spoke, "Dominant ideologies create norms while resistance to them is contained in the classes. You don't contribute to that, though, if you're constantly at war with what I've been taught."

He nodded, said, "It's like, I want to lead everyone on how to act and be and then again, it would take up so much of everybody's time, it would be so much better if prejudices weren't ingrained, but something like peace was." He detached himself from speaking and gassed the weed string trimmer's choke then pulled back three times. It kicked alive with a thrum and he began to tear apart the grass around the part of the lot to the left of the house.

There were and had recently been an explosion of wealth that had led to increasing inequality and a lack of affordable housing for those without high-paying jobs. People like to know that when trouble comes, there is somebody that will own it and act for everybody.

As a warning that I would be leaving to work soon, I pressed compliments into Cecilia's hair.

She sighed out, "No need to be affirmed about the things I already know I can do and have confidence about."

I retracted from my embrace, "What, baby?"

"I said," she stated, "that if I recognize my self worth, do you still stick around?"

I retracted ever further from her, increasingly anxious as I stared at the person from which those words had come. In a hot, tumultuous state, I left that morning and continued everyday to work early in the day and come back when the sun gave no more light and the spaces of ground I was working became too dark to remain at. I worked hard for the greater good everywhere but my own house. There, and only in my bedroom, could I look out the window at the pale skies overhead and act just as insignificant as I was to that ever-pressing future.

I asked Tre's advice on an early spring day spent outside working and he snorted, saying, "You know Shellie?"

I shrugged my shoulders, thinking of all of the phrases I had heard from her making a nice feminist manifesto, "Yeah, and?"

He said, "Been trying at her for five years."

"You know what she would say to that?" I asked him, thinking of the person she was.

"What?" He asked, attentive.

I said, "She would tell you that that's a creepy load of bull and that you're no protagonist for chasing after her so long."

"No," he put up his hands, "I get her, man. I wouldn't bring her flowers. She would tell me I should be dead rather than them. I wouldn't ask her on a date, she gets to do that. I don't do creepy stuff, I just show her my personality, you know, I'm easing into it. Really taking the long road."

"No wonder you didn't want to move out of Lower Bottoms!" I mocked, throwing a dirt clod his way. He nodded and I had to ask, "Why are you dating other girls?"

He looked at me, then let his eyebrows fall as he said, "I like a lot of people, all right?"

We went back to work until he asked, "How was your luck with girls in the past?" I looked over to see him nuzzling his hands back in the ground to make room for a start.

"In boarding school we had co-ed art classes," I told him. "Looking back I can tell this one girl really liked me because she wouldn't show her work to anyone but me."

"And?" He prodded.

"She once cut off her own hair and taped it to a pencil when I stole all of her paintbrushes," I said, finding it less funny now that I was an adult.

He chuckled and asked again, "And?"

"I told her the things that were wrong with them, mostly." I said with a grimace.

"Ryan Hull!" He laughed aloud, "What, specifically, would you say?"

"I said that her sunsets looked like the apocalypse."

He shook laughing, "You were messed up, man."

"Not as selfish as you," I told him, "by going after Shellie, a girl that doesn't want a guy."

"I want to be with a girl like that because it means I would really mean something to her. She has to really know she likes me if she wants to be with me. I'm not just some guy. I would be the guy for her. Talk about something else."

I looked around ourselves, thinking that the people living south of the lot were predominantly younger white kids and Latina families. They were some to the Northeast that were the same way, up until the tubes and the highway bisected them. For a mile or two north, the five or ten blocks that started at 7th street formed linear segments of schools, churches, corner stores, and housing. That's where I saw Charles sitting and, also where Edna had lived.

"Cecilia's mom lived where mostly black people live," I said, pointing to the area I had just been thinking about, "Even though she's Mexican."

"Yeah well black people don't say, 'You can't live here unless you look like us.' That's a white people thing." He laughed as he said it while still looking down with a frown embedded on his face.

I became selfish, I suppose, when it became apparent in the first weeks of spring, that Cecilia didn't like me working so much and often. Tre told me he heard her moan and sob when I left and I could hear crying faintly one morning. I had left to work a new plot a few blocks up from 8th street when I remembered to go back for my sunhat and gloves. Tre's aunt had recently moved back to Atlanta for his Grandma and he was prone to stay watching movies to no end in his room instead of helping out.

I ran up to the house when I heard the faint, mumbling crying at the crosswalk. I paused at the door, knowing she would quiet when I opened it. I knew she would stifle her sobs but I wanted them to walk along my mind and leave footprints to what I could have done.

As the wood gave way from the handle and my feet were racing up the stairs, her muffled mouth breathed softer and I heard no more crying. I opened the door to see the comforter and sheets wrapped up like soft-serve ice cream. I opened a gap in them and found Cecilia's face. I kissed it and wrapped my arms around her shoulders.

"What is it?" I asked, "Did I do something?"

"In my dream I couldn't look you in the eye," she told me, looking at me now without blinking.

"Well," I began, lamenting my poor use of opening wording. I was baffled.

She sniffed, "You deserve to be told, too, but I won't. I'm scared and know you won't leave me. Instead you'll get upset and I'll try my best not to do the same. You'll ask me questions and we'll cry and maybe we won't be able to breathe and will start hiccuping, we'll be so upset." She was the epitome of the image she was painting, "Our pain will be mutual, if I do. For now, though, I'll bare this weight until it ruins me."

I took a look at her, to photograph her in my mind, strongly facing me and herself at the same time. "I love you," I thought and told her.

"I love that you love me even when I hate myself. After being someone I hate. I love that you know when to back off and not take offense. Even when nothing at all can make me feel better, you remind me that I'm not a bad person. Being wrapped up by you centers me," she whispered into my collarbone now, "for the same reason I was willing to be with you and make it work, I'm telling you I am unhappy."

"Am I making you hate me?" I asked, looking down without disturbing the way she held onto me.

"You're not growing, you're just stressed and scared," she said at me.

"I'm beginning to fear being too well understood while I'm growing," I said as emotions roared in my ears.

She said nothing

"Do you hate me?" I asked.

"It is because I love you," she said.

"Am I making you hate me, though?"

She shook out her head of curls and said, "It's not, 'I love you but you're making me hate you.' It is, 'I love you, but you're making me hate myself,' that is true."

I dropped my hands and took a step back, "Then you shouldn't be with me."

She looked at me, perplexed, "You're leaving me?"

"I don't want to hurt you by being with you," I pleaded with myself as my words formed and sprung out of my mouth.

"You're leaving me because you're hurting me?" She asked.

I looked at her as if her face would forever hold less brilliance, her words less song, her body less grace, "When there is danger, I'll throw the things I want to protect as far from me, so that they can't get hurt."

"That's not just you that does that," she said, wiping her palms against her thighs.

"I don't want to lose you," I said.

"You shouldn't pick a flower up if you love it," she whispered.

"You pick flowers all the time!"

"For medicine!"

"Your medicine," I threw up my hands.

"The Brugmansia seemed to work."

I looked at her speculatively, then stopped thinking, "I won't fight."

"You are fighting."

"Gandhi was a lover, not a fighter. I'm a fighter."

"Osho said that about the flower, not Gandhi."

"Well, he was a lover, too." I pleaded, "I'm not! I'm sorry! It's just not how I was raised!"

"Don't raise your voice," she looked terrified, her eyes pleading with me, now. "I can't take yelling."

"I'm not yelling!" I told her sternly, maybe aggressively.

"I'm out of here," she said. "We're not taking a break or going to get back together." She was grabbing things. Important objects of hers. Things I didn't need but wanted around to know that she was there.

"I'll fight for you," I said, holding her arm.

"But you won't love for me," she said brusquely, "and that's what I'm asking."

I set my jaw.

"And you cannot do that," her eyes had frantically searching mine, but now they were frantically searching the baseboards and undone, re-salvaged, mahogany steps until she was walking down them. She touched the stained glass she had done with regular craft supplies before she opened the door. I understood her point enough to clutch my forearm as I stood squarely in the upper portion of the hallway.

The rest of the day hurt like I had shaved off my fingertips to avoid arrest and was debilitated instead. I couldn't put my mind to anything and, like a ghost visiting old haunts, went to the cafe.

I ordered solemnly, drank my coffee and went to talk to Chloe at the radio station, realized she only wanted to talk about music, not my relationship ending, and went back to the outside patio to sit alone. I felt like letting loose my lexicon of curse words every time somebody approached, and also wanted desperately to talk candidly with them. Prying for somebody to tell me what I wanted to hear, but couldn't formulate in my own head, I felt lonelier and more depressed the more needy I became.

224

Sol came outside, looking surprised to see me behind her small sunglasses. She began talking about work in the gardens for spring, but stopped herself.

"You're hurting," she said.

"Cecilia and I aren't together, anymore." I told her as she drew near.

"You know I'm a lesbian," she continued, "but I can also tell when men are gentlemen. You are, with or without a girl there to tell you so."

"I never thought a gentleman could hurt a girl's heart." I spoke with an eccentric air of importance, "That's not what I wanted."

She scoffed and said, "Well that's life, sweety-pie," she held my arm, "You don't always get what you want, and sometimes you do."

"Well, I don't think I knew what I wanted with her, in the first place." I admitted to myself that simple truth. "Maybe that's why we failed."

Sol looked at me sympathetically, "Let me ask you if I can take you out today."

"What do you have in mind?" I asked hesitantly.

"You've never been to where this street ends, have you?" She asked, looking distantly at the bright sky.

I said, "All right." Maybe this was what I had come here looking for.

Chapter Fourteen

We drove toward the city on 7th St., toward the ocean and slipped into a part of Oakland that had no housing, just shipping containers, post office parking lots that could double as airport runways, and the great metal structures that lifted the shipping containers. Sol told me stories of her younger days, like how she was attacked by a dog after its male owner had fallen in love with her and what the Pacific Islands were like. She rambled on and let me lap up her stories like a heat-stricken dog at water. We got out of her car after the road turned into a park. She pointed behind us to the silhouettes of Oakland monuments and told me what they meant to her.

Constantly tilting their triangular heads, the shipping container receivers had a moderate likeness to AT-AT walkers from Star Wars. Like the Republic, they represented oppression and industrialization. I thought of the November 1st strike when Oakland workers had stopped working and, for a day, none of these gray beasts had lifted their triangular heads or bowed their rectangular bodies. Nobody had done anything that 2008 day that would give money to the companies that were abusing both workers and consumers. Strikes and marches had been minimized these last few years to make sure rent was paid and food was served.

We continued along the park's meandering sidewalk, skirted by bright green grass and brilliant flowers waving in the wind. We both noticed them but made no comment as we walked on the winding sidewalk until it straightened out and brought us to a stretch hidden from anybody but the boats on the water and people with telescopes in the SOMA of San Francisco. We walked along it casually, without talking of a destination, even though I could see no end to it.

She told me about how people had been forced out of their homes in the 50's, saying, "This was a different place, then, with young people that wanted to raise their grandchildren here and when they couldn't, when they were forced out, they got very upset. The neighborhood changed then. People like me, that are still here and were there during upheavals, are still fighting. Not because we like the fight, but because we hate it so much that we want to protect you, the younger generations, from it."

"I think I know how that feeling of wanting to protect others from something," I sighed, "from something bad."

We relaxed our pace and watched the glittering water together as it lapped forward and drew back. Finally, there was a jetty in the distance. We walked to it, a large grassy one that had embattlements and a WWII fort.

"Do you know something about that war?" she asked me and spoke quickly, "The United States suffered something under seventy civilian casualties from it, but something like seventy percent of the deaths were civilian casualties. That's a terrible number of people that got killed, but few of them were here. And from that war, the United Nations was built! It's amazing what this country got away with, then." I again thought of Einstein and now, Oppenheimer, as well. They were two men very upset about what they had accomplished. Something I had been repressing, that Oppenheimer had said, leaked into my brain. I thought of him hoping people could not see the power of death that lurked in him, that hurt him every second of his existence, and that hurt a countless number of others.

Sol pointed to the embattlement and jogged forward, holding her hands over her pants as she did. I looked over the scene, feeling empty, as I followed her.

I hated myself as walked on like that, feeling vacant and unoccupied after having felt so many confused emotions about Einstein and Oppenheimer. Some unknown beast pulled at my heartstrings, causing my mind to hiccup and sway in a trance I did not understand.

Indifferently, I chose to guide my mind to a problem it could solve. If I was vapid when I was single, I decided, I should never try to date anyone again. That way, I didn't force the people I liked to be with someone as awfully boring as myself. Cecilia had realized it, had realized there was nothing to me, nothing important, that I had been molded by teachers and counselors, and my boarding school administrators and that that had led for me to become the dullest person to exist.

Sol poked my rib and made me react like a pillsbury dough boy when she came out of the fort's restroom. She sighed, looking at it. It was like a cement lighthouse that had been cut down to just two floors.

"I've had a lot of heartbreak before." She said just as the silence between us had grown tension, "I know all of the torturous thoughts your head can make, but don't let the pain make you suffer."

I looked at her, "Thanks, I don't really feel like I know who I am if I can make somebody else hurt."

"That's not you," she said.

I said, "No, of course not. Not at all."

"That's what you did, though, yes." She said and I struggled to put those seemingly contradictory thoughts next to one another, "You loved, though, didn't you?" She asked, delightedly opening her arms and letting the sea-breeze pick up her clothes.

"Yes," I giggled, but it was so light the wind picked it up and carried it off. "Yes, I did!" I yelled at the ocean, "I was in love and I was loved!"

Sol copied my words but improved on them with more vigor, "I was in love and I was loved!" I looked at her and saw decades of hurt and happiness woven in strong thread under her skin. I had the illusion of thinking I saw deeper scars than were there until she jabbed them with her index finger and told me thy were from the dog bites she had sustained, most certainly as a younger girl. Her eyes searched the linear segments of towers in San Francisco and for the first time in a long time I did nothing as I searched them with my eyes, too.

"Now about this with Cecilia, what is the biggest problem?" She asked.

"I guess that I... You know that I should ask her, herself, Sol."

"Do I?" She asked while looking directly at me, "I don't think so. Because I think you were in a relationship and that is the union of two people's character, in my

229

book." She rolled her feet on the ground, "Years later you might look at how it ended and say, 'Yezus I did some things that I really don't like now.'"

I said, "Well I never think I'll admonish myself and everybody ends things differently."

She smiled and I again spoke, "Everybody is different."

"Are you going to find out what she wants to do?" She said on our walk back inland.

I reacted quickly with words, "I shouldn't if I want to protect both of us."

She looked at me gruffly, lips over-lapping, then spoke, "You're not the kind of man to scare a girl."

"Not at all." I thought for a moment, "We do need to find out what we both need."

"Without being too direct," she said.

"Are you telling me to be ambiguous with her?" I asked.

She shrugged and only when we got to her car, a light blue '89 Mercy B, did she let the words in her mouth fumble out, "I'm telling you how to listen."

We pulled away from the park and drove back the way we had come.

"Uh-oh," she said as our car approached two hot rods in front of us. They were both getting larger as we approached, then simultaneously darted from their positions.

"If you want to see drag racing here," she said, "there it is."

We both shook our heads and sighed on our way back to the cafe. It was afternoon now and the blue of the sky was opening for the colors of the impending sunset.

I was worried about running into Cecilia at the cafe as Sol parked next to it, so thanked her for taking the time to make sure I got a positive outlook. I opened up the fence into the lot and started working, moving piles of firewood and splitting it, even though the cold season had left us, taking apart old chairs, re-aligning all of the chairs that were out there; I did anything I could that kept my body moving just below its fastest speed. There was a fire-pit where Leonard's body had fallen into the earth and I thought about his bones, burned in the landscape. I turned my attention to the chicken coop, re-enforcing decaying parts of it with wood I had just salvaged. Working in the breezy wind that lifted the garden's many leaves felt like being bound to the image of paradise when your insides are in turmoil.

I grabbed dirt and plants haphazardly when I started to garden. Anxiously, I tried to undo mistakes, only to make more. Maybe because my mind was other places, I didn't have it coordinated with my hands. Tall kale stalks were breaking on their stems, chamomile was bruising in my hands, and I pulled things out when they were already past the right stage and were inedible, now. The vegetables were basically all on the precipice of being ready, but with that knowledge can no new trust in my future. I would give most of them to the community members interested and make ramen noodles and nothing else at home. It was silly to think I needed nothing when I was alone, but there was truth to the illusion.

When the prick of sun was gone, I went inside to the shell of a house. I saw Tre in his room and we sat together.

"We've failed," I announced.

He scoffed, "At doing what?"

I explored the thought and re-stated, "I've failed."

He again asked, "At doing what?"

"I was too stressed and scared to make a difference," I sighed and tried to focus my attention on the movie he had been watching.

"There's a good sort of stress," he offered.

"What is it?" I asked.

"There's eustress. Good stress. Eustress is short term, tangible, and with a return to relaxed state. When you're stressed but not scared. I think that's what you went through."

I thought about just how little I had told Tre about Leonard. As I did, a violent, visceral image of Leonard's bones breaking in his jaw. A cold shiver of worry ran down my spine. Tre raised an eyebrow and looked at me, perhaps sensing my tremor or simply waiting for a response.

"I don't think it was the good kind," I said.

"Want to tell me what happened?" He asked.

"Irrelevant," I said.

"If it is, in truth, irrelevant it had no bearing," he said, "it looks like it did."

"I'm actually beginning to get the sense that my perception of it was," I searched for words but couldn't finish my statement.

He interjected on my thoughts, "It doesn't follow. You have no valid argument from this to that about it? Then yeah, it's irrelevant."

"What is, then?" I asked, lost.

He said, "Your failures, apparently."

I mused, watching the television blink erratically at us images of cyan hues, "Exploring new ways to get around what has already been created."

"Why weren't you okay with what was there?" He asked.

"I didn't like thinking that it was making people die," I thought longer, "that me doing things could make people die."

"Well, first of all, the systems are fucked. Black people talk about the systems of oppression that kill them and take away their money, but you, a rich kid with the world smiling on you, can't move the systems, either. They're there and they suck the living soul out of everybody but the people controlling them."

I nodded, halfway attuned to the pit in my stomach lurching into my spine, brain, heart.

He continued, "You can't hold the world's burdens, or even this community's, on weak shoulders. Plus, we haven't even harvested the vegetables in the gardens. Go for gold, baby, it's right there."

I sighed out a reply, "The garden isn't going to change the big rotating cogs set up years ago that keep crushing humanitarian thoughts and free-thinking and throwing some cherry tomatoes at it isn't going to stop it."

"Yeah, but the juice might just rust it up a bit," he tried, grinning.

"Might," I said.

"Listen to yourself, you're anchoring to this result you have in your head," he said, "that isn't right. Classic human mistake, really."

I was watching the t.v. more than listening, "Oh yeah?"

"Just because a truth can be denied does not mean it should be," he said to me, picking up a pillow and squeezing into it as the blue light from the t.v. touched him.

"I just wanted to take the inhumanity out of humanity, man," I caught myself saying, "I just get the nagging sensation I have not, nor will I do that."

We both sighed exhausted with everything, even ourselves. If we couldn't change anything as individuals and everything was set up to hurt the individual, where could we find hope?

He looked at me and added, "I have to keep hope for a future not through reason, science, and progress but one of barriers, hate, and suppression. What else is there?" He shrugged with me, frowning.

"I was never before sure that there was a glass ceiling and ninety-nine percent of people hit it, but I am now," I said.

"Don't give up trying to break it," he said.

"I don't know how to start," I said.

He shook his head and frowned further.

Chapter Fifteen

Tre and I lived in the house, starting an affinity for the music in the area as well as the gardens. We hosted shows once or twice a week for local musicians of all types. One of our friends laid down a fresh rap about the Lower Bottoms, which held me aloft for a few weeks. The shootings and gangs from Leonard's sect were still around, tearing up the neighborhood any way they could. We distributed food from the garden to everyone interested. The reward of smiles and thanks made me feel self-serving.

It's not enough, I would think with my eyes peeled back and my head abuzz in the hours when sleep should have gripped me. My good intentions are not enough, just as Cecilia predicted. They say you fall in love with people that remind you of your first love, for the rest of your life. If that is true, I'll be spending the rest of my life in love with girls with bouncing, curly black hair and an affinity for new-media street art, and had an undeniable tie to my past, which were quite rare. I didn't meet anyone that interested me, but when I did, my throat caught in my chest and I hoped I would really be meeting her all over again. When I happened to walk behind someone that looked like her, my heart was pulled like a marionette and I thought, for a moment, that it would be her. I found out from people at the cafe that she had moved back in with her dad, a man I had never asked about.

I spent the mornings staring out of the window like I had done when she had lived with me. The day would wrap its hands around my neck in the morning and, if I let myself breathe deeply during it, the rest of the day would not wrap its knuckles so firmly around my throat. The summer was creeping in on Oakland. Fruit and squash slowly pushed themselves out of flowers and cloudy weather all but near ceased. If the season and town hadn't been commercialized and industrialized to the point of spitting up crude oil in the cracks of the sidewalk, it would have been beautiful to me. I saw its beauty in reflections of people like Sol and Charles. They had been there before I was born and would be buried there after they were dead. They were the reason I kept trying everyday. The reason I wouldn't rush away on a train or in my car. They were the reason I had so much hope for the community and knew it didn't need me to survive.

"Like I said," Sol mused again, "the community loves itself, it won't let anything too bad happen to it. Your presence here changes it, though, every person that cares can have that affect. You're not here for yourself, you're here for West Oakland."

I nodded solemnly, thinking about what that meant if I didn't believe Oakland wanted me here for it.

Outside of my house, I saw one of Carlyle Bruisyn's cronies talking angrily to a girl that hung around the corner store. I started approaching, ready to tell him off.

"Hey, you don't know what's going on here," he interrupted me as I raised my voice to ask him what was going on.

"I don't think you know how good my vision is, because what I saw," I said, "was you, roughing up this girl."

She looked at me, saying, "Thank you,"

"She was hitting me first," he said.

I said, "I don't care, I'm not going to watch that happen."

The two were separate now and he looked to me angrily, "You didn't see anything."

"I saw what I saw," I said, adding, "and didn't like it."

"You can go back to your momma now, kid," he said to me.

"Go back to daddy Carlyle," I replied hotly.

The sun pulsed on me when I said it and I felt my eyes adjust to quickly watch his hands move and his posture widen. His hand clawed over the top of the gun, snapping it back and letting it fly forward as he flicked his thumb and pressed his index finger to the trigger.

I thought about bleeding out, scared and sad, in the street, and quivered.

"This is your house, isn't it?" He asked, throwing the but of the gun toward the gate. I nodded and he snickered, "I won't get in trouble for this. Show me in."

I looked behind me quickly, then back at him. Taking him in the house meant exposing Tre to the violence. I dropped to my torso, planting my hands. I swept my legs and kicked his shins. I watched him tumble as I stood up.

His hands splayed open to catch his fall and he dropped his gun. I listened to it clatter as I envisioned his blood filling the cracks of the cement. I knew I didn't want to pick up his gun and use it against him. I picked up his gun, releasing the clip and letting the bullets hit the ground.

I saw his eyes flicker to me as he realized what I had done. I was standing over him, preparing for what I would do next, when I saw his eyes look behind me. I followed his gaze to register a hand, a balled fist of a hand, hitting my face. Before I could pull back, a frigid feeling from my abdomen pushed me backwards, into the grasp of the man I had pushed down.

"On the curb with his head," I heard someone say, or was it "melon" instead of "head"? I would like to remember back on it as them all being quite serious, but it was so mechanical to them that they let loose a few jokes and chuckles about me as two men positioned my body on the street. I scrambled with my legs, endeavoring to escape, but they threw me on the curb. They turned me over, pulling on a shoulder that felt very detached from my body. I shriveled up from the pain.

Carlyle Bruisyn stood on the sidewalk and lifted his foot quickly and forcefully against my face when one of the men said I was ready. Carlyle and the men left with the man that had held the gun at me after they had split my face between boot and curb.

The body I had held was gone, the one that had been drugged by Cecilia and her yellow Brugmansia flowers was gone. On que with the unfurling of my bones and blood, my subconscious opened, showing me the things that I had done while under the influence of the bell-shaped flower. The disgusting body that I had hallucinated and killed Leonard Kiljun with was dying, now, and it was purging the guilt it had carried. I felt no unity with the world, I felt like I was going to a hell, laughing as I realized I had already dreamed up my own Heaven with the man I had killed and all six children he had killed there. If only it had been real, they would be waiting for me. It hadn't been, though. It had all been an illusion, as I had said to my dad, it had been a head trip.

I laughed to keep from crying because If I cried, I might repent and seek forgiveness. The guilt of finding drugs in my blood and blood on my hands made me sick. Flashes of him dying at my own hand perturbed my self-concept gradually as I sat there, grasping for happiness and finding none, then deeply as the full extent of the knowledge struck me.

I laughed to keep from crying because the wound over my belly made me sick, too. It looked like a gash I had seen in pictures of whales after they had been knifed or the cross sections of the Earth, layered and colorful. I saw the top layer of skin, like the Earth's crust and a sheet of muscle, not unlike like the mantle. Below that, it didn't look like the Earth core, it looked like a bunch of worms and slugs. Like snakes, I thought as the image of Leonard Kiljun's body being overwhelmed by them was replaced with my hands spraying blood and dismembering him.

I kept laughing as I buried my right fist into that gash because the pain of it made me feel like compression would suppress it and held onto my right shoulder with the other, which felt harrowingly loose. The haze of yellow surrounding my vision

239

panicked me as I lay there dying and I worked quickly to hold onto the thoughts and feelings that I felt slipping from my grasp. I felt like a car swerving on the road; my trajectory had changed, yet I knew I needed to keep on going the path I had been on. Was that because I didn't want to die and was failing to side-step it, failing to move at all, or as a more daunting alternative: I was more than ready to wash my hands and die after killing another human being.

I had never known what I was going to do, but now I wished that I had had limits. If I had only wanted to teach him a lesson, I wouldn't have done to him what I did. If only I had dealt with him before starting to see Cecilia.

My life didn't unfold as I lay dying, the darkness of it let my brain cast light on the insidious way I had ended Leonard Kiljun. That yellow bell flower's kiss had claimed my mind that night and day. That yellow flower and I had claimed his life and now mine was gone, too.

Deservedly, I was going to be gone. If I had struggled against the pain, I may have lived. If I hadn't embraced it, ashamed of what I had done while alive, I may have suffered but gotten through it. But my hand pressed deeper into my wound, trying to pull out my gut. I poked with my index finger and pulled with my middle. I tore at my insides like they were the cause of the world's pain and of its injustice.

My story didn't deserve a spot in the news and my name wouldn't be on a white cross on the lawn of the San Pablo Boulevard's church. It wouldn't be there because I had grown up. I had grown up privileged, everything in my lap for me to build success, and I had failed, then fallen.

www.ingramcontent.com/pod-product-compliance
Lightning Source LLC
Chambersburg PA
CBHW021232130626
46554CB00004B/1450